Trust in the Unexpected

Trust in the Unexpected

GUNNEL LINDE

illustrated by Svend Otto S

Translated from the Swedish
by Patricia Crampton

A Margaret K. McElderry Book

ATHENEUM 1984 NEW YORK

Library of Congress catalog card number 83-73165
ISBN 0-689-50300-8

Printed in Great Britain
First American Edition

1

Katie was walking home alone. Lou, who sat beside her at school, had gone off in another direction. She would rather walk home with their teacher, Katie thought. She lugged her school bag along, weighed down by four books.

"Lou doesn't want to walk home with me. She's afraid someone may come and tease me. She thinks I've got such funny eyes. And I have, too," Katie said to herself. "Lou doesn't know that I can cross my thoughts. She thinks I can only cross my eyes. But I can do both."

She looked over her shoulder at the school. It was in its right place, and almost all the children had gone home.

If I flashed my eyes a bit, Katie wondered, would the school fly up in the air?

She put down her bag and looked at the school again. Then she closed her eyes and pressed her knuckles against them. When she had kept her hands there for a little while she began to see red and green clouds which turned into golden stars. Katie knew she ought not to do it, that it was not good for her eyes, but on special occasions she did it all the same.

"May stars rain down on the school and the whole roof explode!" said Katie aloud. Then she felt sorry for the school. Perhaps she would really prefer it to be there in the morning, with their teacher and Lou inside it.

"It can stay where it is," she said, and opened her eyes.

The school did exactly that, and Katie walked on.

Anyway, I've got Swan, thought Katie. Perhaps she'll draw something for me. But Swan won't be coming out of school for a long time.

Swan was Katie's big sister and her real name was Sylvia Wanda.

"But then there's Joey. *He* needn't bother to come home," thought Katie.

Katie's big brother Joey was ten, a little older than she was.

"If only Mum's home!"

But Katie's mother was a mailwoman and would very probably be somewhere out on the streets with her heavy mailbag.

"My bag's heavy too," thought Katie, hoisting it up.

She was aware of Lou, a long way off on the other side of the school, skipping along beside teacher.

Perhaps she's turning round and waving to me, although I can't see her, thought Katie. She turned on her heel and waved at the school, walking backwards. No Lou to be seen, of course, but Katie waved and smiled so that it could be felt right through the school building.

A long, long way off by the fence she saw someone watching her. It was only Jump-jump whose real name was Mike.

Katie went on her way. Jump-jump had been in Joey's class when they started school but later he had had to move into a special class because he could never sit still. He kept bouncing up and down in tiny hops like a sewing-machine needle. Sometimes he got up on his seat at school and jumped with both feet together until someone told him not to. Sometimes he left his desk and hopped round and round the classroom, or so Joey said. Nowadays he had taken to leaping round the streets at top speed so that no one could keep him company. He didn't want company. Or perhaps he did, although he

couldn't stop? Sometimes he used to hop beside Joey for a while, taking small hops so they could look at each other. And now had she really seen Jump-jump waving back at her?

Perhaps he thought I was waving to him, thought Katie.

She walked a little further before looking round again. Jump-jump was standing in the same place. He had been standing still for some time, oddly enough.

I'd better wave again so that he'll be sure I wasn't waving to someone else, thought Katie. Otherwise he might be hurt. After all, he's never waved at me before.

She waved.

Jump-jump put his hand up a little way and waved back from where he was. He jumped up and down once or twice, then came bolting past her at high speed and disappeared like a streak round the corner.

Katie went on walking home, hoping that at least Swan might be there, doing her homework. People doing homework are no good, of course, because they are thinking about something else and are scarcely there at all, so you still feel lonely. They might not even notice if there were burglars banging round the house. At the very worst, even having Joey at home would do. When he was around they were usually so busy squabbling about who was going to get the last piece of cake or the last lick of jam or the first crust on the loaf that Katie's fears had to wait. Katie knew she was going to be afraid of the dark in broad daylight as soon as she got inside the door, but it could not be helped. Now she had reached the middle one of the terraced houses, the one with the little gate that you could step over, and the lilac bush.

Once home, Katie slammed the door behind her so that all the burglars and ghosts and nameless horrors would know she had come.

"Here I come!" she shouted, to give them a chance to leave.

No one answered. The hall just looked at her. The kitchen and dining-corner did not say a word. The stairs to the first floor held their breath. All the rooms were hiding behind each other, obviously afraid to answer.

Katie took her coat off, shouting, "Hello! Now I'm going out again!"

So that no one would think she was still inside, she opened the outside door again noisily and slammed it shut. Before anyone could catch her she had slipped into the bathroom and locked herself in. She was safe there.

Katie adored the bathroom. It was so small and so brightly lit. Not a single dark corner! No one could possibly come up behind her without her knowing it, and the lock on the inside was the best thing of all. She hung up her coat on the dressing-gown hook and closed the lid of the lavatory. She could live there for ever and a day, whiling away the time. The best way to do her homework was to read aloud, Katie thought, then you could be certain that you really were reading. She began in a loud voice – but bathrooms aren't good places for reading. Your voice echoes and booms. Better to listen . . . but there wasn't a sound.

Katie began reading again as if she meant to go right on. Then she made a sudden stop and listened. If anyone thought they were meant to get away with tiptoeing round outside the bathroom unnoticed, Katie would trick them. Surely she had heard something? Yes, she had!

Katie could clearly hear someone tipping over the sugar-bowl in the dining alcove.

Katie didn't believe in burglars, not really. She knew she was just being scared of nothing. But now she had heard something; it was not her imagination! The sugar-bowl had fallen over.

This time there really is someone there, thought Katie. What shall I do?

At first she decided to go on reading, louder still. Then she thought she would shout for help through the drain hole at the end of the bath. It was quite possible to be heard clearly along the pipes to the neighbour's bath if one lived in a block of apartments. Unfortunately this was a terraced house and there was no one at all beyond the hole, except perhaps a wood-louse.

Katie picked up the lavatory brush, held it behind her back and unlocked the bathroom door with a firm hand. She stepped out and said, "I give myself up!"

The cat on the table looked surprised. He was the one who had overturned the sugar-bowl. Katie let herself go and howled with laughter. "Silly Tango! Don't be scared!"

Katie managed to make herself a sandwich and take a bite of it while the laughter lasted, but then the uneasiness came creeping back. She let Tango come into the bathroom with her. If they were together there was no need to be afraid. The dressing-gown could be rolled into a cat-nest in the bath. She made a nice dent in the middle for Tango to lie on but he stood by the door and mewed to be let out again.

"Be quiet! Dracula will come and eat you up!"

At that very moment someone came to the outside door! Mum? Swan? Joey? thought Katie. But the door did not open and no one rang the bell. It was just the door handle making a noise.

"Someone is trying to break in," Katie whispered in the cat's ear.

Tango looked sympathetic. He still wanted to get out.

"We could probably manage to tiptoe past and rush out through the garden door," whispered Katie. "Don't be frightened. It's not Dracula. I was joking. It's probably only a robber."

This time she took a towel with her. As she opened the bathroom door she flung the towel over into a corner on the other side of the hall. If anyone was getting ready to shoot he might believe that Katie was over there where the towel had landed. That was how they fooled detectives on television. Katie rushed to the garden door and thought she would never get it open, her hands were so clumsy.

Tango watched her for a moment and then jumped into the kitchen sink to lick up drops of water.

Cats are never kidnapped, thought Katie.

She rushed the length of the terraced houses and rounded the corner. There was no one following her. Katie was furious with herself.

"How many times are you going to be so frightened, stupid idiot!" she said to herself. "Now I'll go straight down the path and ring at our own door! If the burglar is there I shall look him straight in the face and tell the police what he looks like!"

But the door bell was already being pressed. There stood Katie's two-year-old brother, whom Mum called Charlieboy. The babysitter was standing not far away with the other children, waiting to see that someone let Charlie in. Instantly Katie was transformed into Charlieboy's sensible big sister, not the least bit afraid.

"What a sweet little Dracula!" said Katie, as she let him in.

She decided that she would never be frightened again in her life. Or not today, anyway. At least, not for quite a few hours.

2

Katie took off Charlie's woolly cap and tried to get at his zip-up suit.

"Stand still and let me unzip your zip," she told him.

But Charlie was determined to twist himself round and stretch out his arms for the cat. Tango was wise enough not to come within reach. When

the zip had been pulled down and the sleeves were off, Charlie heaved himself through the opening and went after Tango without waiting for Katie to get his legs out.

"Wait, wait!"

Charlie plumped down on all fours and began crawling after the cat. Now he was crawling out of the suit as well.

"There you are, you see," said Katie in a motherly voice.

The telephone rang. Katie jumped. If it was some villain ringing up to find out if Katie and Charlie were alone in the house, he was not going to get away with it!

"Hello, this is the police station," said Katie.

"Well, what are you doing there?" Dad laughed. He was calling from the far north.

Katie's father was an engineer who spent his time driving a train away, and then driving it home again all night. Or the other way round. Often he was so far away when his working day was over that he could not come home at all and had to sleep in lodgings somewhere. In that case he generally telephoned. Katie calmed down, inside and out, as soon as she heard him. She told him about the bathroom, the towel and little Dracula and laughed so hard she nearly choked with laughter. Dad was laughing too, up in the north.

"What are you up to now?"

"I was just thinking of cooking something," said Katie.

"What kind of something?" asked Dad suspiciously. "Tell me what there is in the cupboard and I'll tell you what to do, otherwise I'll just sit here worrying."

Katie took the receiver over to the cupboard and the refrigerator and let it look at bags and packages. There was plenty of macaroni and stale bread. And flour and chocolate powder. A little butter and an end of cheese. An almost full bottle of milk and a few eggs sat in state inside the lighted refrigerator.

"Pancakes," said Dad. "That's the best thing. But it would be better if I stayed on the 'phone all the time. Don't put the receiver back! Get down the mixing bowl and one egg. Break the egg into the bowl for a start. I'll tell you what to do then."

Katie laid the receiver down on a pot-holder while she fetched the bowl. She had to climb up on the counter because the china cupboard was too high. But it was quite easy. All she had to do was to pull out the drawers, the bottom one further than the top one, making them into a staircase. Then she could climb up them and get out the bowl. She did not break it on the way down, either, because she put it on the counter first.

Now for the egg. Katie took it out carefully, very carefully, and held it in her hand. There lay the egg, hunched up, silent and unsuspecting. Katie felt shy of the egg. She did not want to break it on the edge of the bowl. She stood for a long time looking at it. Crack it, what an idea! When eggs were so wonderful! Neither round nor oval, but roundoval. Absolutely white, too, without a single mark!

Meanwhile Charlie had taken charge of the tele-

phone. He didn't say a word, just stood holding the receiver. Now he was narrowing his eyes to peer into it. Katie took the telephone away from him and Charlie yelled.

"I'm so sorry for the egg," Katie told Dad. "It's horrid to have to break it. Couldn't I break a cup instead? There might be a chick inside the egg that would be upset."

Dad groaned from the far north. "Eggs don't feel anything. There isn't a chick inside, I promise! Hurry up now! It's expensive making pancakes on the telephone. Why is Charlie yelling?"

"Because I won't let him hold the telephone," said Katie calmly. "But the egg is so beautiful . . ."

Crash-splash she heard. Katie turned. Charlieboy had broken the egg into the top drawer. Now it couldn't be anything but a pancake, in all its glory. Katie took the spoons out of the drawer and then pulled the whole drawer out so that she could empty it over the bowl. Then she had to pour milk into the bowl and whisk the egg at the bottom. Dad told her how many cups of milk to put in. At last the mixture was thick enough to stretch from the wire whisk just the right way.

"Hang up now," said Katie. "I'm going to fry the pancakes, so I can't hold on to the receiver."

Dad was suffering. "You mustn't have the frying pan too hot, the fat may catch fire and you might burn the whole house down . . . In fact, don't fry the pancakes at all. Let Mum do that. Oh, why did I think of this idea! It's dangerous. Open the front door so that you can run out if it starts to burn . . .

But how about Charlie . . . ? No, I forbid you to fry pancakes. Did you hear me?"

"Ye–es," said Katie reluctantly.

"If anything happens it will be my fault! You'll go and forget to turn off the hot-plate and it will melt, I know. And you'll burn yourself! Oh, why do I have to drive a train? Why do I always have to be a hundred miles away from you? What am I going to do?"

"Calm down now, calm down," said Katie, just the way Mum did. "Everything's going to be all right. I shall be as careful as anything."

"No!" shouted Dad from the far north. "Wait, don't fry them until Mum gets home. She'll be there soon enough!"

" 'Bye 'bye," said Katie.

Now she really did feel like a mother. It's no good being so careful that you dare not do anything at all, she thought. If you take such care of yourself that you're wrapped up in cottonwool, so to speak, you might hiccup yourself to death, as Mum used to say. Katie felt as if she must dare to make pancakes now.

So she dragged the big frying pan on to the hot-plate and turned it up to 3 before putting the butter in. Then she chased the pat of butter round the frying pan with a knife and spooned some of the pancake mixture in as soon as the bottom of the pan was shiny. At first nothing happened. And then – still nothing. What happened finally was that all the pancakes fell apart when she tried to turn them over. It was hopeless! As soon as she put the spatula under the edge of the pancake, it split. And if she did manage to get the spatula under the middle of the pancake it broke apart when she was about to lift it up. It was turning into a scrambled mess except for one pancake she left in the pan until it was black. There was not much of the mixture left in the bowl. Katie scraped out the frying pan again, rubbing and scrubbing away at the bottom so that not a scrap should be left in it. She had four flat plates on the work counter with tattered little bits of pancake on each. The perfect pancake, the one that stayed quite round, was to lie on a plate of its own without any unfortunate accidents underneath it, she planned. But the perfect pancake had not been made yet.

Katie put more butter in the pan and whisked the batter hard. Hocus pocus, abracadabra! Once again she tried to spoon the right amount in, not too little, not too much. Oh, now the frying pan looked like a pale golden floor, right to the very edges. That was how the batter was meant to look!

"Don't lift it, don't lift it!" Katie told herself.

Finally the pancake lost its shine and began to look more like a pancake than a lake. It hissed and released air bubbles at the side. The edges bubbled gently.

Katie waited and waited. Now or never!

She took a second spatula out of the drawer, one that was not dirty already, and poked it under the edge. Wonder of wonders, it slid in under the pancake – no disasters – oh, horrors! The pancake was going to break again! Katie drew the new spatula out and waited. The spatula was still shiny. Then she eased the whole spatula in again, lifted the pancake and tossed it over. The perfect pancake had been made! A single, completely round, unbroken pancake had come out of the frying pan and landed on its own special plate.

Katie was so happy that she danced around the kitchen. It didn't matter now that all the rest were just as scrambled and messy as before. She gave Charlie some scraps of pancake to eat with his fingers from a bowl on the kitchen chair.

When Dad 'phoned again to forbid her to touch the stove everything was ready and waiting. Katie had laid the table for the whole family, put the pancake fragments in an oven dish to keep warm and set the successful pancake in the place of honour. There were glasses of milk poured out and the sugar-bowl and the jam jar. There were knives and forks, lying there looking expectant. Now somebody must come home and eat the pancake! Swan should have it – no, Mum should.

Katie ran upstairs to fetch her five teddy bears and sat them in a circle round the plate with the proper pancake on it: Big Teddy and Middle Teddy, Bearbear, Fluffy and Woolly.

"Now you're not to move," Katie told them. "You're going to have your own plates with pancake scraps on them."

Charlie tried to look over the edge of the table.

"What about eating up my best pancake all by myself?" said Katie. "No, never! Everyone's got to see it first."

Katie had to go to the lavatory, so she took Charlie with her. He might be a danger to the pancake. But before Katie had finished she heard the outside door shut and someone coming in.

"Swan! Mum! Wait for me!" called Katie. "You mustn't look at the table!"

She pushed down the handle and jumped off the seat simultaneously.

Beside the dining-table stood Joey.

"Where is the pancake?" Katie screamed.

Joey chewed. "I've eaten it all up."

"NO!" screamed Katie. "You weren't supposed to! You weren't allowed to!"

"But Mum had made it for me!" Joey insisted.

"She hadn't. It was my pancake. I made it."

"So what?"

"It wasn't for you."

"Pancakes are for eating," Joey persisted.

He knew nothing about the only perfect pancake in the world.

"Not mine. Ooooh! Now you've ruined everything. You nasty, greedy toad! It was going to be a surprise!"

There was no batter left. Katie would never make such a wonderful pancake again.

"It was, too," said Joey. "It was a surprise for you to find that the pancake had been eaten. Disappointed, eh?"

Joey didn't care a bit about all the work Katie had done and now he was teasing her as well. Katie rushed at him and tried to hit him but Joey wasn't concerned. He knew he was stronger. Before Katie could do anything, Joey had grabbed both her wrists and was holding her firmly so that she could not move. Anger went to Katie's head as if she were a shaken bottle of soda water. She screamed with rage, but Joey thought that was funny. He laughed in her ear and pushed her away. When Katie tried to catch

him, to bite him and smash him to bits and hammer him into the ground, he just jumped behind the table and began to throw bears at her. He threw Big Teddy straight into her arms, Middle Teddy hit the wall and might easily have died and Bear-bear flew into Katie's face. She got his arm in her eye and it hurt. She could scarcely see where Fluffy had gone, she could only hear him whimpering – he must have sprained his claws! Weeping, Katie gathered up her bear babies as quickly as she could and hid them underneath her bed. When she came back for Woolly, who was her favourite, Joey had opened the door and was holding him out by one ear.

"Let go of Woolly!" Katie screamed.

Joey threw Woolly into the middle of the road, where the traffic could run over him.

Katie rushed out and heard Joey close the door behind her. Tenderly she lifted Woolly, brushed him and kissed him. She dried her face on his face and comforted him at the same time. Joey would never touch him again. She tucked Woolly under her sweater and pushed him down into her belt. Then she looked at the front door, which seemed to be calling, in Joey's teasing voice: "You can't come in! I'm not going to open!"

Katie marched over to Joey's new bicycle, which was leaning against the fence, gleaming. She took it by the handlebars and pushed it away from the house. The bicycle obeyed Katie like a dream. It made no resistance. Katie walked quickly all the way down Park Street, turned the corner by the park and raced downhill with the bicycle. It almost ran away with her, but she held it firmly by the handlebars and mastered it. At the river bank there were planks for bicycles to run along, but Katie trudged through the sand. Up on the jetty she went, and out towards the diving board. But Katie did not dare venture on to the springy board with the bicycle. It could so easily push her off. She just gave it a shove, straight into the water, which splashed up in all directions.

"Stay there!" shouted Katie in her clearest, loudest voice.

And then she went home again.

She did not care if anyone had been watching her, up there at the crossroads.

3

Joey was expecting Katie to start beating on the door but when she didn't he thought she must be waiting for him to open it, to see if she was coming.

He made himself an enormous cheese sandwich with bits of cheese filled in like a jigsaw puzzle until the butter could not be seen at all. But not a sound from Katie.

If she can wait, so can I, thought Joey, switching on the record-player in the living-room. He had put on the old record that Swan always played when she was unhappy. Then he lay on the sofa and bit luxuriously into the sandwich. Swan usually backed Katie up and helped her as soon as he tried to tease her. If Swan came home now he might tease her a bit at the same time.

"Yesterday, yesterdayayayayay, sulky bayay-be," sang Joey, loud enough to be heard outside. He was singing so that he would not hear Katie trying to get in. Surely she was trying? When Joey had finished his sandwich he got up and stole over to the door in the hall. He could not hear Katie but she would have no idea that he was there either, the music was thumping and howling so loudly.

Joey peeped out of the corner of the bathroom window. No sign of Katie from there. Then he crept down the hall and opened the door a crack. If she tried to grab the handle he would shut it again at once. But nothing happened. Joey was getting bored. He opened the door quite wide, calling, "Come on then!"

No Katie. Katie was not outside the door.

Joey went back in and stood in the middle of the kitchen. The table was askew and one fork had fallen on the floor. He picked the fork up and straightened the table. Katie was always getting annoyed about nothing. If you were hungry you had to eat, didn't you? How was he to know it was her pancake? Joey finished setting the table to rights so that everyone could sit round it, and added butter and a jug of milk. He made himself another sandwich. Then he went in and fetched Katie's bears from their hidey-hole under the bed and set them elegantly round Katie's plate. She could have the table laid as she liked as far as he was concerned, as long as he did not have to starve to death. When she came back he would tell her that it was a good pancake.

Someone opened the front door. Joey turned and tried not to look as if he were teasing, but it was only Swan.

Deep inside Joey thought Swan was beautiful. Her fair hair and white skin shone in the dim light of the hall as she hung up her coat. It was Joey who had started calling her Swan, when he was little and could not say Sylvia Wanda. Now everyone agreed that it suited her. She was always so calm, extraordinarily calm right inside, whatever was going on around her. Sometimes she seemed to be all alone in a different landscape behind a window frame. She could slip past Joey in the kitchen without looking at him and walk round eating her sandwich as if he were not there. If he tried to tease her she usually teased back by being calmer than ever. Her patience was at least ten times greater than Joey's. That is, as long as he didn't use her records. Then she would flare up at once, looking really threatening when she went for him. Fortunately the record he had been playing was finished.

"I've laid the table," said Joey.

Swan was not listening. She put her drawing pad on the counter and pointed. "Have a look?"

Swan had been at the riding school, drawing as usual. He saw long rows of arched horses' necks and horses' legs in clusters or at exercise, filling the whole sheet.

"Why have you drawn nothing but legs? Couldn't you put them on horses?" Joey commented.

But Swan refused to be upset. She stood there, smiling at something quite different. On the next sheet there was a whole horse and a dirty little boy in the left-hand corner. Swan smiled at the boy-squiggles which were nothing like anything that Swan usually drew.

"Who did that one?"

"Alec did. He always draw boys like that and he's

got a little sister who draws almost as well as he does. Her name is Jane."

"Was that Alec at the riding school too?" asked Joey.

"Looks like it. Did you think he was a ghost rider who sat at home and drew on my paper by remote control?" said Swan promptly.

You could hear that this was one of the days when she might sink to a little bickering if he really pushed her hard enough.

"Alec has drawn a little boy on every single one of my horse pictures. His boys are going to look after my horses, he says. Next time he's going to bring Jane and his own drawing-pad."

"Obviously he likes you," said Joey angrily.

"Perhaps I like him?" said Swan.

"I thought you liked Peter Moore. You have for the last hundred years."

Swan did not answer. She was looking through the other drawings of boys.

"He draws girls too," she said. "Quite big girls with breasts that wobble. And sad little women and big tough blokes. He has done one of his little sister that's exactly like her."

"Little sisters are no good," Joey stated.

"Where is Katie, by the way?"

"How should I know?"

Swan looked up from the drawings and stared Joey straight in the eye. "You always have to squabble. What have you done to her now?"

"Nothing. She started it."

"People who live in glass houses shouldn't throw

stones! I know very well who usually starts it. You go out and look for her, in case she's sitting crying somewhere."

"I haven't the faintest idea where she went!"

"That's your worry. You've got to try and find her. Alec stands up for his little sister. He even spends some of the breaks with Jane at school."

"I don't care what Alec does," said Joey, going into the hall. He tried to look as if he were just going to ride down to the playground on his new bike.

"Don't eat up all Katie's pancakes. I'm hungry too," he said from the doorway.

Swan turned over the page to look at a drawing of a new boy and took it up with her to the record-player in the big room. The house was on several levels with two rooms on each. A lot of time was spent running up and down stairs to whichever room you wanted, rather like a canary bird hopping between the perches in its cage. This time Swan took the stairs in smooth leaps which turned to a dance step on the next floor. A little bit of belly-dancing and a little bit of jiving and a little rock. The first tune on the record fitted in straight away with the easy rock movements. Then she practically sat on Charlie who was snoozing in a corner of the sofa.

Joey returned to the front hall, yelling. "Swan, have you seen my bike?"

"Certainly. It's red and it's got horns like a metal reindeer. It's got a plastic bun that you sit on and a whole lot of pointless knobs. What's the matter with it?"

"It's not outside."

"Where did you put it?"

"I put it by the gate."

"Oh, you probably left it at school!"

"Of course I didn't."

"Did you lock it?" asked Swan.

Joey did not answer. He remembered at once that he had not locked it. But after all, he had put it by the front gate. Surely people wouldn't come and take bikes that were standing at their owners' gates? How dishonest could you get? Dad had told him a hundred times over that he must lock the bike everywhere he left it. But did *everywhere* include your own front garden? Could *everywhere* mean even the patch of grass outside your own front door? And anyhow, Dad hadn't yet bought him a bicycle lock.

Joey went out again, sorry that he had talked to Swan about it. The bicycle could not have gone! His brand new bicycle, which Dad had bought for him barely a month ago . . . Could he possibly have forgotten it at school and walked home without remembering he had it?

Joey knew that was impossible. He could no more have forgotten one foot and hopped home on the other than have forgotten his bike. He remembered every yard he had travelled as he rode home. All the same, he set off towards school at high speed – he had to do something.

At the corner of Park Street he all but knocked down Jump-jump who was standing there, hopping up and down.

"Out of the way! I've got to get my bike!"

Joey rushed past without looking round. Jump-jump rushed after him, keeping alongside for a while. He and Joey used to run races with each other in the school yard during the early days when they were in the same class. But now Joey was going so fast that Jump-jump was left behind. Joey didn't even look round or seem to notice that Jump-jump was there at all. Jump-jump slowed down. He could not stop, but he remained on the same spot, bouncing up and down restlessly by himself.

Joey rounded the supermarket, slid to a halt in front of a shopper, jumped to one side and shot across the grass which no one was allowed to walk on. He thought he saw his mum a long way off – someone walking along swinging a mailbag like hers – so he ducked between two rose bushes with his arm across his eyes. No one must ask why he was not bicycling.

The school yard was absolutely empty. True, there were one or two bikes in the stand, but not Joey's. He would have recognized his a long way off.

Who could have taken it? Nicky? Mac? Could Ian Brook have borrowed it, or someone he didn't know at all? Victor, in the class above his? He *had* to get it back again!

Suddenly Joey saw his father in his mind's eye, his father who was driving down from the north at the speed of an express train. What would Dad say; how angry would he be?

Slowly Joey began to walk home again, peering closely at every bicycle owner near and far. No one had his bicycle. He checked every bike leaning against the walls of houses, both locked and unlocked. None of them was his.

Whoever had pinched it was certain to take it out some time. No one would keep a bike indoors. I shall get it back, thought Joey, if only I've got time.

He was keeping a look-out for his mother, who had reached the supermarket and gone in to shop. She had not far to come now and if he let her go in first she wouldn't notice whether he was bicycling or walking. It was no good talking about it before the bicycle had been found. He saw his mother walking calmly along, lugging her bag, not looking round at all.

Suddenly Joey noticed that Katie was also walking along the street, halfway between him and Mum. He would have to slow down even more. Katie had no coat on. She was just as she had been when she was locked out. Hadn't she seen Mum then? She must have – Katie was looking straight ahead – and yet she was walking as slowly as a beetle on a patch of glue. Why was she doing that? When Mum stopped to change hands, Katie stopped. When Mum walked on, Katie stood stock-still where she was.

Go on! thought Joey, get into the house, don't look over here!

Katie set off again as if Joey had her under remote control.

At the door to 43 Park Street Mum put her bag down and tried the door handle.

This was the moment. Joey hid behind a parked car as Mum opened the door and disappeared. Only Katie was left and when Joey came out she had reached the door. They were quite a long way apart so she should get there long before him, but she stopped with her hand on the door-knob.

What are you waiting for? thought Joey. Open it!

Katie turned, gazed round her in all directions and then straight at Joey. Now she had seen him. They stared at each other while a car drove past and a plane faded into noiselessness on the other side of the roof. Katie clutched the door-knob again as if she were frightened of him, but Joey reached her before she opened it.

"Not a word about the bike!" he said. "Someone's pinched it. Promise you won't tell Mum, not for anything!"

"Yes," whispered Katie, so quietly that he could scarcely hear her.

4

When Joey and Katie came in Swan was sitting at the table with Charlieboy on her knee. She was feeding him with Katie's pancake pieces in bite-sizes. Charlie was helping her with his fingers. If the spoon was in the way and his mouth was full he tried to stuff his pieces into Swan's face. They were both pretty sticky and the whole house smelled of pancake and soup.

"Where's Mum?" asked Joey.

"Here I am," said his mother, coming out of the bathroom. "What did you want me for?"

"Nothing," said Joey vaguely. "I was just wondering."

He took shelter on the other side of the table.

Mum had been out for several hours with her mailbag and looked windblown.

"Lovely to come home to a house smelling of food," she remarked. "What have you been cooking now?"

"I've made a leek and potato soup with milk," said Swan. "It's simply delicious but of course it won't do for Charlieboy. He only wants pancakes."

"I believe you," said Mum. "Are you all right, my little piglet?"

Charlieboy flung out his arms and grasped Mum's hair to pull her face towards him. Mum succeeded in popping a kiss on a slightly less sticky spot, but that was not good enough for Charlie. He wanted to rub her nose and be stuck to her for ever.

"You can have him," said Swan kindly.

"It was Katie who made the pancakes," said Joey unexpectedly.

Mum took a bit of pancake from Charlie and ate it. "Mmm, it's good. Who taught you to make pancakes?"

Katie walked past the table and started up the stairs. "Dad. He 'phoned."

Her mother and Swan looked up.

"You have been working hard, Katie," Mum said. "There are enough pancakes for us all here!"

"Aren't you going to eat?"

"They all broke in bits. I don't want anything," said Katie, going to her room.

"What does it matter when they're going into your tummy anyway," said Mum and then she called, "Come and join us, otherwise it won't be any fun."

But Katie did not come back.

"She did make one pancake that was round," said Joey.

"What's happened to that?"

"I ate it," said Joey.

"I see," said Swan. "That's what you were arguing about. I thought there was something."

"You always side with Katie. You're never sorry for me," said Joey.

"No, I'm not," said Swan. "We can't be sorry for you when there's nothing to be sorry for you about, can we?"

Joey filled his mouth with pancake fragments and frowned at the butter dish. He had to remember not to make a slip and start talking about the bicycle. Talk about unfair! What was an eaten pancake to a stolen bike?

"I don't care a bit if he did eat the pancake. I don't mind about it," came Katie's voice all of a sudden. "It doesn't matter."

"Good. Fine. Done! Finished!" said Mum, who thought that was the end of the matter. "The main thing is that there was a whole, beautiful, perfect Katie pancake here. That's all I need to know. Next time you can make pancakes for Katie, Joey."

Joey didn't answer.

Up in her room Katie buried her face in her hands and tried to choke back the sobs. Pulling Woolly out from under her sweater, she rolled over and covered her head with the pillow.

Mum and Swan went on banging around downstairs as if nothing awful had happened or ever could happen. Swan was serving her soup as a follow-up to the pancakes and the plates clattered about.

"Do come down and have a little soup at least!" Mum called from downstairs.

Katie lifted the pillow a fraction to hear but pulled it down again. She was not going to sit looking at Joey who no longer had a bike. Surely he would be

able to *see* that she was thinking about a boy's drowned bicycle, and she certainly didn't dare go near Mum. What if I couldn't help talking about it all? thought Katie, and that made her cry even more.

She could hear Mum joking with Swan and Swan joking with Mum down there in a different world where the plates clanged in the sink and the water ran noisily. All they cared about was whether Mum was going to stay at home and put Charlie to bed or if Swan could do it instead so that Mum could go and see the ballet at the opera house.

"I like people who talk with their whole bodies. Best of all when they've got strange, transparent clothes on which float and waft about as they move," said Mum. "Dad thinks the ballet is the most boring thing in the world, he says they just 'scissor their legs'. So it's best if I go there and have my fill of dancing when he's not at home."

"Let her go," Katie heard herself shouting. Katie didn't want anyone to be around when she was thinking about the bike.

"When's Dad coming home?" asked Joey.

"Not until Friday," said Mum. "But I've got a ticket for today."

"You go off then," said Swan. "What would you have done if I hadn't said yes?"

"I would have rung the theatre and asked them to throw the ticket out of the window," said Mum.

Mum came running up stairs to her bedroom. She opened cupboard doors and pulled out drawers, then there was the sound of shoes being tossed aside. She was busy turning herself into a beauty, just like Cinderella, Katie thought.

"Now don't get twisted, you wretched scarf," she heard Mum say.

She'll be coming to say good-night soon, thought Katie.

Quick as a flash she tore off her shoes and jeans, pulled back the bed cover and wriggled down under the blankets. She dried her face again on the pillow and for safety's sake she pulled out the lamp plug so that it would not switch on.

"There, now the necklace has broken." She heard Mum's voice. "I'll take Katie's beads instead. They'll look pretty."

She stood in the doorway in her best dress made of three different materials. Her shadowy face and the front of the dress which was quite dark were turned towards Katie and only her eyes shone a little, but Katie could see that the black, pink, white and amethyst-coloured beads she had strung together were hanging round her mother's neck. They gleamed a little where the light on the stairs caught them and there was a glimpse of green and flowery silky pleats.

"Is this all right?" she asked Swan.

"Watch out you're not dragged on to the stage with the dancers, the way you look!"

"I'd grab the chance and leap about just like them," said Mum.

She had Katie's teddies in her arms as she stepped into the dark room.

"Here's Big Ted and here are Middle Bear, Bear-bear and Fluffy. There you are."

Katie pushed Fluffy and Bear-bear untidily down by the wall and took Big Bear in one arm and Middle Bear in the other. Woolly was tucked under her chin. Then she closed her eyes so that her mother could not see what she was thinking.

"Sleep well, darling," said her mother. "I shall send you everything I'm looking at by thought transference. Don't be surprised if you dream about dancing girls."

Katie hugged her so hard that it hurt her arms but then she let go hastily. She could not hear what else Mum and Swan said, only the slam of the door at the end. Mum had gone.

Katie went on lying there, quite dazed with misery. She heard Charlieboy screaming furiously when he discovered that it was Swan and not his mother who was going to put him in the bath. Soon afterwards Swan passed Katie's door with a freshly bathed Charlie under her arm. Katie had not been able to have a single thought except "bicycle!" all that time. Desperately she dived right under the bedclothes and began to remake the bed from the inside as she always did. No one could make a bed just right for Katie, only she herself. The coverlet had to be tucked in tight right down the sides and round the corners without the slightest little gap or gleam of light from inside. And there were to be no sheet corners sticking up your nose in Katie's lovely underground home. It had to be as solid as a fortress with only one entrance. When she was quite certain that she had tucked herself in she wriggled out of her sweater and socks and pushed them out of the opening. Then she crawled up again like a rabbit and arranged herself among all her teddy bears. It was then that she saw Joey standing by her bed.

"Don't say anything to Swan," he whispered. "I am going to slip out and look for the bike. I've got to find it. I've got to have it back before Dad comes home."

Before Katie could answer Joey had left the room.

"Where are you off to?" came Swan's voice from below.

"Back in a minute!" shouted Joey.

"Half-past-eight at the latest!" Swan cried quickly before the door shut behind him.

Katie lay there, afraid to think. She did not want to think about the bicycle any more, the poor bicycle! Nor about Dad, poor Dad fast asleep in the north, certain that he had given Joey a bicycle which he still had. And she would not, would not, think about Joey wandering around in the streets and never able to find it.

Katie's tears began to flow again and she could no longer cry silently. The tears burst from her eyes and ran down her chin. She was shaking all over. Swan came out of her bedroom.

"Are you crying?"

"No-o-o-o," cried Katie.

"What is it?"

"Nothing. Everything's so awful . . ."

"What kind of everything?"

"Don't know."

"Are you afraid of the dark?"

"No-o-o. Ye-e-es . . ."

"There's nothing to be afraid of here, not here and not now. I'm not thinking of leaving you. What are you afraid of?"

Katie clenched her teeth, closed her eyes and tried to stop crying but then she couldn't breathe. She had to snort and snuffle.

Swan pulled up the sheet and dried her face but when more tears came Swan let her long hair fall round Katie's face so the two of them were alone together under the hair. She put her arms round Katie and held her gently.

"There there," said Swan. "Now we're living under my hair, just you and me. Nothing bad can happen to you here."

"Let me go," sniffed Katie, clutching Swan tightly. "I want to crawl under the coverlet and never come out again, not even tomorrow. It's not fun being alive."

"Who says that?"

"You said it yourself! That's what you said when Peter Moore left."

"Ah yes, I see," said Swan. "Yes, I very probably thought that, but it doesn't feel like that any more. I've turned Peter into a lovely little puzzle picture in my memory. Sometimes I take him out and have a look at him. What does he really look like? Where is he now? I think. And then I put him in the top drawer of my mind so that he won't get lost! I grew tired of being sad. Now I'm happy at the slightest thing, all by myself."

Swan's calm voice caressed Katie's ears, her breath fanned Katie's damp cheeks like a southerly wind. Swan's forehead rested against Katie's forehead so that they must almost have been thinking the same thoughts.

"Don't cry! You'll be feeling better soon," said Swan.

Katie gave a sob, but the tears gradually stopped running and suddenly she sat up straight.

"I've got to go out," said Katie. "I want you to go with me."

"Are you cracked! I can't leave Charlieboy, can I?"

"Then I'm going alone," said Katie.

"You can't go out in the dark. You're afraid of the dark!"

"Yes, I've got to!"

Katie wriggled out of the bedclothes and the pale curtains that were Swan's hair. She pulled on a sweater and skirt and went slowly downstairs, where she picked up her coat and pulled on her boots.

"Stop, I won't let you go out alone!" called Swan. "Wait till I see if Charlie's asleep."

Katie did not wait. She flew out of the door and hurried in the direction Joey certainly had not taken.

It was lighter out than in. The sky had not switched off yet and only the trees were dark, though the street lights had come on. Katie ran as fast as she could towards the river. She was already losing her breath at the top of the hill but on the downhill run she picked up such a speed that she could not stop. Her legs were running away with her. In the heavy sand on the edge of the swimming pool she was brought to an abrupt halt and almost fell headlong.

Katie climbed on to the jetty and looked down. The water was completely black and smooth – no sign of a bicycle. She went back to the bank and began to wade out into the water. At first she did not

notice that she was wearing her boots and coat but very soon water was pouring over the top of her boots and her coat began to float out behind her. Katie moved resolutely on, but she knew that it would be no use trying to swim in boots; she would have to turn back.

She put the coat on the jetty, and her boots in the sand. Katie sat on the end of the jetty, holding on with both hands. How would she ever dare dive down to the bicycle?

Suddenly she heard Swan's voice a long way off. "Katie, where are you?"

Swan was nearby and would soon be with her. Katie jumped in. She sank nearly to the bottom and popped up again without drowning, but it was no use, the bicycle was not there.

"What on earth are you up to? Have you gone stark, staring mad?"

"Yes, I have," said Katie, "stark, staring mad!"

She gave a miserable little laugh.

"What are you doing here in the middle of the night?"

"Swimming," said Katie.

"With your clothes on? Now I've heard everything. Have you gone crazy? What's the matter with you?"

"I had to come here," said Katie.

"Who said so?"

"It was that Olive. A girl I know . . ."

Swan took Katie by the arms and helped her to put on the half-soaked coat. They emptied the boots and walked home, Katie shuddering so violently she could scarcely walk. Swan walked in silence for a long, long time as if hoping that understanding might come if she did not speak. Katie walked in silence too, until at last Swan began to ask about Olive.

"Is it anyone I know? Or Mum?"

Katie didn't think so.

"Tell me about Olive!"

"She's the most horrible person," said Katie. "Stupid and nasty and nuts. She's got no sense of respectability. I don't like her but she always orders me about. She said I had to go and swim."

Swan gave Katie a sideways look. "It's not called a sense of respectability, it's called a sense of responsibility."

"Oh," said Katie. "What does it mean then?"

"It means knowing what you shouldn't do."

"Olive doesn't," said Katie, as she pulled off her boots at home and unwound the soggy coat from her legs.

Swan gave her an extra-thorough looking over and put her in a hot bath. Katie made no protest; there was nothing she could do now but sit in the warmth and not bother about the bike any more. Olive had taken over.

5

The next morning Joey and Katie were both in a hurry to get to school.

"Well, did you dream about ballet dancers flying through the air and collapsing in a heap on the floor? I sat there thinking about all of you as hard as I could while I was watching. I thought I would telepathize everything back to you so that it would come out of our television up here. And then Swan would have been able to watch it when she switched it on," said Mum. "Didn't you see some poor peasant girl dying of love while her princely lover was bounding through a make-believe forest?"

"No-o. I have to go now," said Joey running downstairs.

Katie was standing by the door, wearing her wrinkled coat which they had put on the radiator overnight.

"Well, are you coming?" said Joey.

He nearly pushed her out through the door.

"We didn't have time to watch TV here," said Swan. "Charlieboy got in a furious temper when you had gone and bit the washcloth whenever it came near him and screamed like a screech owl. Joey went out and didn't come back until half-past-ten, although I told him to be here no later than half-past-eight, and Katie was weeping like a tap, too. Then she went off to that swimming place on her own and jumped in the water with her clothes on . . ."

"What?" said her mother. "Is this true?"

"Oh yes. I don't understand how you can have the courage to be a mother . . . how you manage to live through it."

"It's no use stopping once you've started," said Mum. "You just have to go on, whether you can manage or not. I took a chance and I do the best I can."

"Yes, but all children are crazy at times."

"No, they're not really," said her mother. "They do what they have to do. Everything depends on something else, if only one can understand."

"Then you explain to me what good sound reasons Katie could have had for jumping in the water in the middle of the night with her coat on," said Swan. "She blames it on someone called Olive."

"Tell me from the beginning," said her mother.

After Joey had made sure that Katie was out of Mum's and Swan's hearing he ran to the nearest street corner so that he too was out of sight. No one was going to see that he was not bicycling. But there he stopped and waited for Katie.

"I didn't find the bike yesterday, although I went

round every house. Someone took it in overnight. The thief is probably worried about it because it's so new, or afraid that someone might see it."

"You'll never find it," said Katie quietly.

"Oh yes, I will," said Joey. "I must. I'm going to duck out of school before lunch and go on looking because it might be left outside now when everyone's in school."

"I'll help you look," said Katie.

"If I see anyone using it I'll run after them and hang on tight," said Joey. "Or jump on the back."

Katie walked along, gazing at the ground, without answering.

"Wouldn't it be awful if he was angry and started a fight . . ." Joey muttered.

"It's all right to be angry," said Katie.

"Yes, but not for anything you like," said Joey definitely. "It's my bike, so it's me that can be angry. Not the thief."

"You were the one who ate my pancake and it was all right for me to be angry then," said Katie. "It was your own fault."

Joey sniffed.

"Pancakes – they're nothing to make a fuss about."

"Oh yes they are," said Katie.

Joey swung round and took off in the other direction before they reached the school yard. Katie went on walking, talking to her pretend-Olive.

"The river current has washed the bike away, or else it's rusted to bits. He'll never be able to find it," Katie told Olive. "What shall we do?"

"We could look in the bike-stand in the school yard," said Olive. "There's lots of bikes there, perhaps one of them is like Joey's."

Katie did not answer.

The sun was shining down on the school house and all the gleaming bikes but it was a disagreeable sun, much too strong and bright. It was awful walking across the school yard in the sunshine.

Katie went to the nearest bike-stand and looked around. What did Joey's bike look like? Red with high curved handlebars, but lots of bikes had those. Not all of them were red, however, and many of them were locked.

"We'll take one of the unlocked ones, any old one," said Olive.

"No, no," said Katie.

"It doesn't matter what it looks like, as long as it's just as good," Olive insisted.

"Ye-es," said Katie.

The school yard was full of children, crowding slowly towards the school entrance. There was Lou, looking for something. Katie, perhaps.

"Sshhh, there's Lou," Katie told Olive.

Katie walked in between the bikes, squatting to tie her shoelaces although she didn't need to.

"Hallo, what are you doing here?" said Lou.

Katie had to get up. She did not look at Olive. The school bell was ringing now and Lou pulled Katie along with her. Katie would not be able to return to the bike-stand before the next break, but then Lou wanted to play hopscotch. Katie did not want to play hopscotch because it's difficult to think properly while you're hopping. But luckily Lou wanted to hop first so she had only to watch. Katie stood gazing across at the bike-stands while Lou hopped about, sometimes slightly crossing a line and pretending not to. There was a bike over there with high handlebars, behind the others. Perhaps it was red, too!

"You're not watching! Anyway I hopped in a wrong square, so it's your turn," said Lou.

Katie hastened to hop in the wrong square herself so that it was Lou's turn again. Olive appeared out of thin air and whispered in Katie's ear:

"I think it is red. We must take that one – if only it's unlocked."

But the school bell rang, break was over. Katie ran right round the bike-stands before running into school. She stooped as she passed the bike and took a peep at the lock. It was already broken – and the bike was red.

"No," Katie told Olive. "I wouldn't dare."

Then she was sitting in the classroom with Lou and trying to pay attention. The teacher was writing on the blackboard, her back to the class. Lou went on whispering and whispering, so that Katie could scarcely hear Olive.

"Do be quiet," hissed Katie.

Lou put on her sulky face.

"We've got to do it now," whispered Olive. "The next break is for lunch and someone might ride home on the bike. Now! Now!"

Katie rose on trembling legs. "I've got to be excused," she whispered to Lou.

She wobbled out of the room. The red bike was still standing there but Katie was in such a state that she did not dare try to ride it. She simply pushed it across the school yard under a sun still shining as brightly as ever. But Katie pushed herself along, out of the yard, up the road, round the corner. What should she do now? Where would Joey be?

Katie walked slowly home as if in a nightmare. She could not possibly have run.

"What if Mum's at home?" said Olive.

"Then I'll tell her everything," said Katie, suddenly feeling strong.

"Katie," called Joey.

He was standing on the other side of the road, staring at her. He rushed across the road, stopped dead and gaped, suddenly understanding the whole thing.

"That isn't my bike," he said.

"You can have it from me," said Katie. "I took it for you instead of the other one."

At first Joey said nothing. He looked at the bike, which had the wrong saddle, similar handlebars and no extra knobs. It was red, and that was all.

"It's not a bit like mine," he said.

"No, but still, it's a good one," said Olive-Katie.

"You're out of your mind," said Joey. "Did you break the lock?"

"It was already broken."

"But you did steal it," said Joey. "Just the way someone stole mine! You might be arrested!"

Katie pushed the bike towards Joey. "I want you to have it. Instead of the other. It doesn't matter if I'm arrested," she said.

Joey was flabbergasted. He could not understand why Katie wanted to help him so much, but he did know just how crazily kind she was being. "No, no, no, that's hopeless, we'll both be arrested! I don't want to ride around on someone else's bike, I want my own. Put it back!"

Katie dropped the bike on the street. She just let it go. There it lay in a heap, humming. "I don't dare to. I want to go home to Mum and tell her about the bike!"

That brought Joey to life again. "Don't you dare. She'll tell Dad. I don't want him to be angry. He might think I didn't care about his bike. I'll push this one back and you come too!"

Joey picked the bike up from the ground and straightened the handlebars.

"What if they see us, what if the bell's rung?" said Katie-Olive.

"I'll say we made a mistake; you thought it was my bike," said Joey. "Don't worry, there's nothing illegal about putting bikes back where they came from. Come on!"

They walked back all the way, right to the gap in the bike-stand where the red bicycle had been standing. Just as Joey let go of the handlebars and turned away, the bell rang for lunch.

Joey and Katie looked at each other and sighed with relief.

"We made it," said Joey.

"To the very minute!" said Katie, and she gave a hop. "Now nobody can see what we've been up to . . ."

"We haven't been up to anything," said Joey. "Come on, let's go in. There might be something good for lunch today."

They made their way through all the darting, pushing children and were swept in through the door. There Joey found his class lining up and Katie took her place with her own. They were a long way apart now but Katie couldn't resist running over to Joey for a moment.

"I'm sorry you haven't got your bike," she said.

"Forget it," said Joey. "It's got to turn out right, or else I'll run away on Friday and join the Foreign Legion."

6

When Katie got home from school that day she was almost unable to get through the door. There was someone behind it, and there was a scrubbing and squelching noise from the other side. Grandma was cleaning the hall.

"Who's this cleaning the hall?" said Katie delightedly, in mock surprise.

"It's only me," said Grandma. "I had a feeling that this place needed cleaning as soon as I woke up this morning. I'm so long-sighted that I could see the cat mess under the stairs all the way from home."

"I'm surprised you wanted to come then," said Katie. "It's no fun scrubbing."

"Oh yes, it is," said Grandma. "Scrubbing's my favourite thing, but not everyone knows what fun it is. I asked for a scrubbing pail when I was only eleven years old, a scrubbing pail of my very own and my own scrubbing cloth, for my birthday. And nobody believed me. It's a good thing to like things that nobody else likes because then you can be left alone with your likes. I've always been able to scrub

as much as I wanted to and I get thanked for it too. I know what to do for the best!"

Katie took an apple from the bag Grandma had brought with her and sat down on the stairs to keep her company.

"Scrub your way over here and you can have a bite!" said Katie, holding out the apple.

Grandma took a bite in passing and scrubbed over Katie's foot.

"Can boys run away and join the Foreign Legion?" asked Katie.

"I suppose they could," said Grandma, from over in the corner, "but if they did they'd be very silly."

"Can boys as big as Joey?"

"Not them!" said her grandmother. "They're too young."

"Promise, Grandma?"

"I can't promise because there are always some poor idiots who might think of trying. But what good would it do?"

"We-ll, if something worrying had happened and they were afraid their Dad was going to be angry . . ."

"It would be no better for running away. That's when it really would get worrying," said Grandma.

Katie sighed. Grandma was right as usual, although she didn't even know what Katie was thinking about.

Grandma was wearing an apron over her skirt and her oldest blouse with the sleeves rolled up. Her handbag was standing on the chair in the kitchen beside the bag of apples.

"Have you got a lot of money, Grandma?" asked Katie.

"Yes indeed, I've got as much as I need and I don't want any more. Why did you ask?"

"Because I don't want you to be penniless," said Katie.

She had thrown the apple core towards the sink from the middle stair and got up to pick it up again. Now she was standing right beside the chair with the handbag on it, the handbag gaping wide open. Katie could see inside it, right down to the change purse and the key-ring.

"Do you want anything from the shops, Grannie?"

"Not as far as I know," said Grandma from below.

Katie looked at the zip-up part of the bag, wondering if there was any paper money in there.

"I think I'll go out for a while," said Katie.

"Be sure to dress warmly," came Grannie's voice from inside the bathroom. "There's no warmth in the sun today."

Katie went up to her room to get her coat, but just as she reached the cupboard door Olive appeared. Before that, Katie had only been able to hear her new pretend-friend inside her head, but now she thought she could see her too. Olive had dark hair like Katie herself, only longer. Her eyes stared straight back at you, looking a bit like hard little olives, and Olive always had a little smile, whatever you talked about, as if nothing were really dull or dangerous or silly. There she stood now, ordering Katie about.

"Take Swan's old coat instead!" she suggested.

"What for?" asked Katie.

"Because it's blue, not red like yours," said Olive.

Katie went hesitantly into Swan's room, where the blue coat was hanging over a chair. Swan's check skirt was there too. Katie put on the skirt and coat without asking Olive, feeling that that was what Olive wanted. Swan's clothes did not fit her at all, the skirt hung right down her legs and the coat arms hung down over her hands.

"Just turn them up," said Olive.

"I don't want anyone to recognize me when I go shopping," said Katie, although she did not know what good it would do. But Olive understood.

"They won't," said Olive, "not when you're wearing blue instead of red."

"What if somebody thinks I'm Swan, though?" said Katie in alarm.

"You're not the least bit like Swan. She's beautiful and you look like a dunce's cap," said Olive impatiently. "No one is going to think you're Swan."

Katie went down again and had another look in Grannie's handbag, which was still wide open. Grannie was cleaning the bath.

"Do you want some coffee, Grannie?"

"Not now. A bit later!" Her voice echoed from the bathroom.

Katie got up on a chair and looked in the grocery cupboard. The first thing she saw was the coffee tin and it was heavy, full of coffee.

"We've got coffee," Katie told Olive crossly. "We don't need to buy any."

"What about biscuits?" said Olive.

"There are biscuits there too."

"Shouldn't you have something better than those hard old biscuits?" asked Olive scornfully.

Katie could actually see how crafty Olive was looking. She was going to start arguing soon, Katie realized. It might be best to let Grannie decide.

"Wouldn't you like something nice with your coffee? I could go and buy it for you!"

There was a pause before Grannie answered.

"Yes, do that. Buy something we both like and we can share it," she called after a moment.

Katie snatched up Grannie's handbag and closed it properly. Or was it Olive who snatched it up?

Katie was not sure, but she went straight out of the garden door instead of through the hall and shut it behind her. What if Grannie were to follow her and say that Katie could only borrow the change purse?

"Was that what you meant, for me to take Grannie's bag when she wasn't looking?" Katie asked her pretend-Olive.

Olive nodded.

"What does it matter whether you take the whole bag or just the purse?" said Olive. "It comes to the same thing!"

But Katie knew that Olive wanted to see if there was any paper money in the zip pocket, enough to buy a bike.

"You're nuts!" Katie told Olive.

"You too!" Olive told Katie.

There they stood, both thinking of the same thing. Katie could feel her pretend-friend persuading her to look in the pocket, and Katie was getting angry.

"Well, I'll just show you that Gran hasn't got any paper money there!" said Katie loudly and clearly.

She opened the zip pocket and looked in. There was a lot of paper money, in fact.

"See, she has got some," said Olive. "There's the money. Now do you see why you had to take Swan's coat?"

"No, I don't see . . ." said Katie hesitantly to herself.

"So that no one will recognize you when you go into the bicycle shop and buy a bike, stupid!" snorted Olive.

Katie was so startled when she thought that

through to the end that she had to stop again. She did not want to take Grannie's money, leaving the handbag empty. Grannie, who knew nothing about it and was busy scrubbing away without a suspicious thought.

"I don't want to!" she told Olive.

Olive shrugged her shoulders.

"Suit yourself then, if Joey runs away," she said.

"But what if Grannie's upset?" Katie tried to talk herself round.

"She'd be much more upset if Joey joined the Foreign Legion, and so would Mum and Dad," said Olive.

"Grannie would probably want to lend me the money if she knew I had to buy the bike," Katie said. "I could pay her back with my pocket money. It would only take a year or two. That wouldn't be too bad."

"Of course you could borrow it," Olive agreed.

"At least I could ask what bikes cost," said Katie.

Olive smiled.

"You ask. There's the bicycle shop!"

Katie's heart began to beat faster. The bicycle shop was so close to the food shop that it was almost impossible to pass it by. She opened the handbag and closed it again. The money was still there and there was no one around who could stop her from going in and buying a bike. But Katie wasn't going to do it.

"Joey only *said* he's going to run away. He doesn't really mean to join the Foreign Legion," she said. "Joey's stupid. Anyway, he's too young."

"What's he going to do then, when Dad gets

home? Is he going to tell him someone stole it?" asked Olive.

Katie went all quiet inside when she thought of Dad and Joey face to face. Neither Olive nor Katie knew what to do next.

"In," said Olive at last. "We're going into the bicycle shop. We must!"

As Katie opened the door a bell rang, ting-a-ling. There were lots of shiny bicycles inside, row after row along one wall, like horses in a stable.

Many of them were red, many had the same bent handlebars as Joey's bike and two had saddles like his.

The salesman came out.

Katie took three quick steps towards the door as if she thought she might manage to get out. She was turning her back on the shop assistant when Olive stopped her.

"No nonsense now! If someone asks who was here buying a bike he'll say: 'A girl in a blue coat.' You haven't got a blue coat, everyone knows that," Olive whispered. "No one will know it's you."

Katie stood, as if frozen to the door knob.

"What did you want?" asked the salesman behind her.

"I want to know how much a red bike with those high handlebars costs," said Katie.

The salesman named a huge amount of money without a blink.

Katie was so pleased that she beamed all over her face.

"Thanks, it doesn't matter then," she said. "That's much too expensive."

"Wait a moment. You might buy it on an installment plan . . ."

"Goodness, no," said Katie before Olive could interfere.

"Don't you want a bike?" the salesman called after her.

"No," said Katie, stopping. "Unless you've got a boy's red bike for free, of course."

The salesman went back to his office irritably, without answering.

Kate skipped on to the grocer's shop.

"How stupid can you get?" Olive whispered in her ear. "Why didn't you stay there and take it on the installment plan? A small amount of money might have been enough to start with!"

"Because I don't want to take Grannie's money!" said Katie. "You are not going to make up my mind for me, so pay attention to what I'm whispering!"

At that very moment Olive seemed to have been blown away on the wind. Katie had to stop and look around, as if she might be able to see where Olive had gone.

Katie hurried into the shop and bought doughnuts and macaroons for herself and Grannie. She paid with coins from Grannie's purse and closed the bag properly.

"Where are you off to with that big bag?" said Mrs Nettleton at the cash desk.

"It's Grannie's handbag, I've only borrowed it," said Katie.

"Isn't Grannie afraid to let you out with her entire fortune?" asked Mrs Nettleton.

"No, because I take such care of it," said Katie.

Kind Mrs Nettleton was one of Mum's fellow conspirators who helped keep the family in order. She knew straight off what they hadn't got at home and what they needed. An extra key to the garden door lay safely in her cash drawer in case they should all lock themselves out at the same time.

"Hurry home now, so that villains don't get it off you," she said to Katie.

Katie hurried home with the macaroons and

doughnuts. She hadn't thought of anyone but Olive trying to get hold of Grannie's bag. What would she do if some big noisy boys came and tried to take it from her? Or a real handbag-snatcher? To be on the safe side Katie began to walk alongside the nearest elderly man, who looked severe and impressive. No one would dare to touch her there. He looked at her askance.

"Where did you get hold of that handbag?" he said loudly.

Katie jumped.

"It's Grannie's. I've been shopping for Grannie!"

"Crazy people!" said the man, talking to the air. "Trusting children!"

Katie ran off, looking round as she went. She could not see any thieves at all, back, front or sideways, only Jump-jump darting towards her from a long way off. He could not possibly be a thief! He waved, but Katie ran off at top speed anyway, so fast that even Jump-jump got left behind.

Grannie was sitting at the kitchen table resting when Katie came in. The coffee was already made.

"You're just in time," said Grannie. "Just look at your clothes! Are you playing at being grown-up?"

Katie fished out the macaroons and doughnuts and laid them on the table. She handed over Grannie's handbag.

"Count up all the money," said Katie. "Here's the receipt from the grocer's."

Grannie looked at the receipt and peered into the purse.

"All correct," she said. "That's just right."

Then she patted her old bag.

"So you've been out and about with Katie," she said. "And I thought I'd left you on the bus. It's lucky you came back."

"Wouldn't it have been awful if I'd taken your money?" said Katie quivering.

"Yes, that wouldn't have been too good," said Grannie. "I need a decent pair of shoes and I'm going to the shoe shop this afternoon, if I don't leave the bag at the post office before then, or chuck it away as I did last week when I was just going to throw out a bag of stale bread. I took the bread bag with me to the bus stop and didn't realize what I'd done until I tried to find the bus fare among all the bits of dry bread."

"What did you do then?"

"The only thing I could do was go back. What your head won't do your feet have to," said Gran. "Were you afraid you might take my money?"

Katie threw her arms round Grannie so that she could not drink her coffee at all. "Oh yes!" said Katie. "I was so afraid I was going to be like Olive. Would you never have talked to me again if I'd stolen your money?"

"You're nutty," said Gran. "I care more about you than about money. Didn't you know that?"

"M'yes," said Katie. "I care more about you than money, too. I didn't take it, although Olive wanted me to."

"Who is this Olive, then?"

"It's a funny sort of best friend I've got. I don't know what to do with her."

"You tell her from me," said Gran, "that she should stop being unhappy for the sake of some money. She'll only get herself in a mess. What did she want the money for?"

Katie did not know what to say.

"Don't you want to talk about it?"

"Olive doesn't want me to," said Katie.

Grannie thought a bit before she spoke. "You tell that Olive that she's the one who should follow *your* example, not the other way round, if she wants to get on in the world."

Katie sighed. If only it had been that simple!

7

Little old grannies can't understand everything, thought Katie. It's only nine-year-olds who know how upside down everything can be. But if Joey would come home, we could ask if we might borrow some money from Grannie for a new bike, thought Katie.

Grannie was preparing mashed potatoes and fried herrings for when Mum came home while Charlie-boy slept. Swan 'phoned from the stables to say that she was going to stay there, but there was no sign of Joey.

"If only I knew where he could have gone," said Mum.

At last Grannie had to go home.

"I'd better hurry before Grandad starts making enquiries for me over the radio," she said.

"Please thank him for lending you to us," said Mum. "Without you we'd be living in a pigsty and the floor would become so dirty that we could grow potatoes on it."

Mum decided to go with Grannie to the bus and look for Joey at the same time.

"Just don't you go and talk about Olive!" said Katie suddenly. "She's not to be talked about!"

Grannie and Mum looked surprised, gave each other a funny look and hurried out of the door. Katie waved after them from her window. Joey should come now, just this moment when they were alone at home and Charlie was asleep. But the street was enjoying its afternoon snooze. No Joey as far as the eye could see.

"What if he's already run away!"

Katie walked restlessly round the house and switched on the radio in the living-room. Perhaps the police would be making enquiries about Joey on the radio and saying he had run away, and Dad would hear about it somewhere up in the north and set off on a long, long trip after Joey. He would be able to catch up with Joey before he reached the Sahara, Katie comforted herself.

She went into Joey's room and stood staring at the empty bed, which looked just as usual, covered with inside-out sweaters and old socks and books. As she watched, the bed began to hump up in the middle. A book slid down the slope. How could that be? Katie looked under the bed. Joey was lying there with an arm over his eyes. She could hear from the sniffs that he had been crying. His knees were poking up the mattress.

"Go away," he said. "Don't tell anyone I'm here!"

"Why not?"

"I don't want them to know I've come home. They'll only ask about the bike and I'm never going to get it back. I know who took it!"

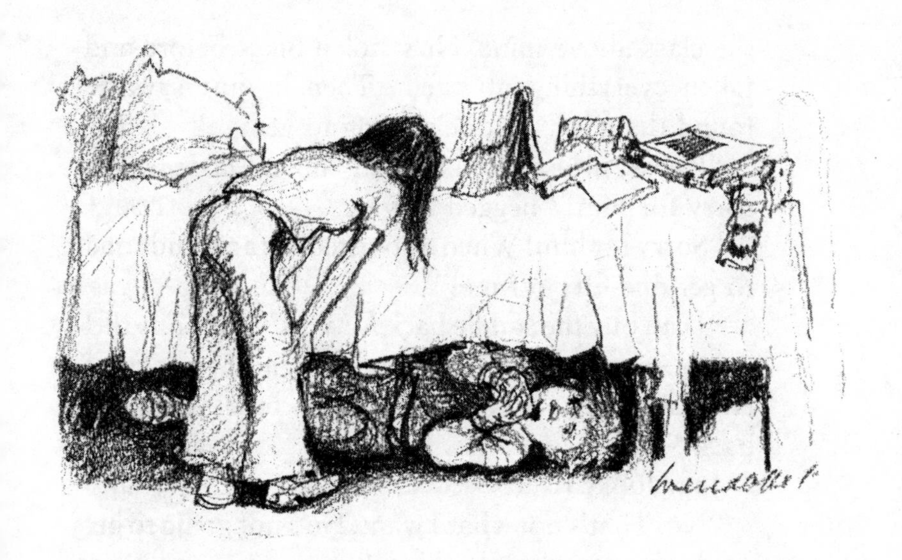

"No!" said Katie, falling on her knees beside the bed.

"Yes. It's a horrible gorilla who shouldn't be allowed on the loose. A really crazy guy, the kind who would do anything. But I'll get him . . ."

"No," said Katie again. "Don't do that!"

"Why not?"

"You might get the bike back."

"No I won't. The bike has been taken to bits! I saw the saddle and bell in school today. In fact someone wanted to sell me the saddle. I tried to take it back but it was no good. I'm going to take a stick to school and hammer him."

"No," said Katie again. "Don't do that, you mustn't! You might be quite wrong. It might be someone else who . . ."

"Oh no," said Joey, "I know that fellow, he's in

the class above mine. He's stolen bikes before and taken everything off them. Then he just says he found the parts. But he's going to get . . ."

"Please, please! Don't do anything. Oh dear, I'm sorry for him!" begged Katie.

"Sorry for him! When he twisted my arm and tried to get one-fifty off me!"

"I can buy the saddle back for you," said Katie. "I can borrow money from Grannie and pay it back later from my pocket money. I can buy everything back!"

Joey looked surprised.

"No. That's not what I want. He's not going to get paid when they're my things!"

"How do you know they're yours? Did he say where he had found them?"

Joey shook his head. The gorilla had said nothing, just swung a bag about with bicycle parts in it. He had stuck it under Joey's nose, and sneered. All he had said was: "Need a new bike saddle?"

"Obviously he knew it was mine," said Joey.

Katie lay down on Joey's bed and put her arm across her eyes as well. How could the gorilla have found Joey's bike in the water? How could he know it was Joey's? Had he seen her throwing it in?

"What's this gorilla called?" Katie mumbled.

"Victor," said Joey from under the bed. "Victor ape cycle-cannibal. I'll grind him to a pulp!"

Katie hung her head down over the edge of the bed.

"Couldn't we ask Mum to talk to him? Or Grannie?"

"He wouldn't care what they said! They would never get near him! He'd be off like a shot!"

"But we could tell Dad, couldn't we? Couldn't I beg him? I could say that . . ."

"No, I told you! I'm going to get every bit of it back myself! I'm going to stay here until I've decided what to do, but then he's going to see stars!"

Katie curled up on the bed. Now everything was just as bad as before. She didn't know who she was sorriest for: the bike, or Joey, or Victor or herself. Or Dad? Dad might be terribly angry with Joey and never want to give him another bike again? What if Joey hit Victor and really hurt him? Or if Victor was stronger and hit back? Would Joey ever forgive her if he found out who had thrown the bike into the river?

"Oh, if only I could help you," said Katie.

"You're the only one who's been nice," said Joey under the bed. "Go and get me a sandwich before Mum gets back, and push it under the bed when no one's looking!"

Katie went shakily down to the kitchen and made a ham sandwich with a lot of butter on the bread. Mum came back just as she was making it but she didn't ask who the sandwich was for, or who was going to have the next sandwich either, or the next. All Mum talked about was where Joey might have got to. In the end she began to make a sandwich for herself. Mum put away the butter dish and piled up the plates while Katie took the heap of sandwiches up to Joey's room.

"Don't you know where he might be?" Mum called from below.

Katie went down on all fours and pushed the sandwiches under Joey's bed.

"No, he's completely disappeared," Katie shouted back.

He had, too. Joey was no longer there. He had decided what he was going to do, and the only thing Katie could do was to look for Joey's bat, which he had fortunately not taken to his room with him. It was in the big cupboard downstairs. Katie hid the bat under the mattress, down towards the foot, so that no one would be able to use it for fighting.

Joey was on his way to the bus stop, determined to run as far as the Easebrook's house. The asphalt was soft and made running easy. Joey's best friend was the Easebrooks' foster son and he would help to catch Victor. Joey was thinking as he ran that if only they could entice Victor there with the bagful of bicycle parts they would be able to prove that they were taken from Joey's bicycle and Victor would be forced to give them the rest back too.

It was obvious from a long way off that Rudolf Easebrook was alone in the house. Rudolf was always in the playroom which was in the basement and had no windows, and he played his drums as soon as his parents went out, and they went out as soon as Rudolf began playing his drums. It didn't worry anyone because the Easebrooks thought that they might have gone out to play bingo three times a week anyway, even if they had not had Rudolf. They knew that foster children sometimes turned out a bit different. Rudolf had a quick temper and if he were not allowed to beat his drums at every possible moment he would become furious at once. Rudolf didn't care whose foster child he was, he just drummed.

Tara-boing, tara-boing, tara-swish-swish-swish . . . Joey could hear.

Joey paid attention: it must mean that the drums were doing well and the whisks were feeling free and easy.

"Ringo!" Joey shouted, banging on the wall. "Open up!"

No one except Mr and Mrs Easebrook would ever think of calling Rudolf, Rudolf. In the neighbourhood he was called Ringo and at school they had called him Mowgli ever since the teacher had read the Jungle Book to the class and Rudolf had asked if Mowgli played jungle drums.

Joey banged as hard as he could on the wall of the house with his closed fist. Over and over again. He knew that the doorbell could never be heard where Ringo was – but Ringo went on drumming. Joey had to sit down on the grass and rest his fist a bit. It looked as if he might be sitting there all evening. At last the drums were silent and Joey ran round to the kitchen window and knocked there; Ringo had come up to get some cooked sausages from the refrigerator. He was tall and pale like a piece of stretched chewing-gum, which is how you get from always sitting in an underground playroom.

"Let me in!" shouted Joey.

Mowgli-Ringo looked up, his mouth full of sausage, and let Joey in. They went straight down to the playroom where the drums stood and Ringo sat down by them again, looking expectant.

"You must 'phone Victor for me," said Joey. "He's the one who pinched my bike. We'll say you want to buy some bicycle parts from him so that he'll come here."

Ringo nodded and gave the big bass drum two blows: ka-bom! "Okay."

"Have you got a telephone book?" asked Joey.

Dang dang dang. Ta ta ta . . . "Over there, on the shelf."

"What's Victor's name?" asked Joey.

Pam pam, ding ding. "No idea."

"Oh yes, you know him, that gorilla who goes around with Johnson."

Bonk! "No!" Ringo banged crossly.

"What's Johnson's name beside Johnson then? And Johnson's dad?"

Ringo began to get involved in his own drumming ideas and did not answer.

Tara-tang, swish, kabonk. Tara-tang, swish, kabonk . . .

"Now just listen," said Joey. "I know someone called Jim who knows Johnson who knows Victor. I can find him in the directory but then you've got to talk to him. He mustn't know that it's me who wants something. Will you do it?"

Swish swish! "Of course!"

Joey found the number and 'phoned around until he got hold of Victor's telephone number. Now it was Ringo's turn.

"Just say you heard at school that he's usually got

bicycle parts and then say that he's to bring a saddle and a handbrake and a couple of new pedals. They've all got to be off a new bike, tell him."

Ringo nodded.

TAN TA-TA . . . "Dial the number then!"

Things began to get rather muddled. Victor didn't want to go anywhere or take the things with him. Then he would come. Perhaps. So Ringo went back to his drums and brushed the big golden cymbals till they echoed.

Ritch-ratch. "So now what?"

Joey began to explain his plan. They would let

Victor in through the main entrance and say the bike was down in the playroom and that they wanted to see if the parts fitted. Victor would not suspect anything because bike racks were often down in the cellar. Ringo would go through the cellar door last and as soon as Victor was halfway down the stairs he would run up again and lock Victor in. Victor would not be allowed out until they had looked in the bag and seen whether Victor had Joey's saddle and other things.

"What?" said Ringo suddenly. Tara-tang tarang-bom-bom ish-dish-dish boing-boing-boing smash! "Let that Victor into our playroom? That's no good."

"Why not?" asked Joey.

"Because my drums are in here of course!" Slabang!

Joey tried to talk Ringo into it – after all, the playroom was the ideal place. Victor would not be able to get out because there were no windows. But Ringo got angry as soon as he thought about Victor possibly breaking his drums or tightening the pegs until the bass drum was ruined. He might even bend the wire brushes.

"Then we'll move the whole set into the bedroom," said Joey.

Ringo banged his drums both loudly and softly. He did not want to stop drumming and he did not want to drum in the bedroom. The neighbours would make a fuss if he tried. But Joey would not give in. At last Ringo agreed to drum in the bedroom if Joey helped to carry everything down again afterwards. When the drums had been carried up there was a ring at the door and Joey rushed to hide in the broom cupboard where he would stay until Victor had gone down to the playroom. Now Ringo would have to open the door and talk for himself without drums.

It was not Victor but his friend Johnson at the door. Victor was standing on the other side of the road with his bag.

"Come on in," said Ringo.

"What for?" said Johnson.

"So we can find out if the parts fit."

"Who's we?"

"Oh, nuts to you and your useless bits!" said Ringo angrily, slamming the door in Johnson's face.

Joey rushed out of the broom cupboard to plead with Ringo, but Ringo already had his hand on the bedroom door and was fiddling with the doorknob. He was red in the face and as soon as he got hold of the drumsticks the outburst came. Joey, equally angry, followed him in and told him off, while the drums exploded with noise. Ringo had not even tried to lure them inside. No one could hear what Joey was shouting and Ringo didn't care. After a while he calmed down, and then both of them heard another ring at the door.

Ringo's anger and his drumming had removed all Victor's suspicions and Victor himself had come to the door. Joey rushed back to his broom cupboard and immediately heard both Victor's and Johnson's voices in the house. They stopped by the bedroom door and talked while Joey held his breath and tried to hear what they were saying. Suddenly an argument broke out, the bedroom door slammed and was locked, Victor yelled and Joey rushed out. It was Ringo who had locked himself in and Joey stood alone, face to face with Victor and Johnson.

"Oh, so you're the one who got us here," said Victor.

"You took my bike," shouted Joey.

"No I did not!"

"You're selling my bicycle parts."

"Am I? Prove it!"

"That's what I'm going to do!" shouted Joey. "I'm going to call the police!"

"My dad's a policeman," said Victor.

Johnson looked uncomfortable. He was peering out of the window.

"Come on, Victor, let's go!"

"I want my bag of parts first!"

Victor began to twist the bedrooom doorknob. Ringo had started to drum again. The whole bedroom sounded like one giant drum, and the door vibrated if you put your hand on it. Johnson, Victor and Joey looked at each other helplessly and it was not until Ringo crash-landed on the top cymbal that they could speak. In the silence they suddenly heard Mr and Mrs Easebrook coming in through the door.

"Hallo Joey," said Mr Easebrook.

"They've taken my bag away from me," said Victor. "With my things in it. Ringo's got it in there!"

Joey was silenced by Victor's name, but he quickly recovered.

"They're not his things at all, they're mine!" he

shouted. "My bicycle parts which he's pinched. I'm the one who should have them!"

"Now, now, boys. Don't let's have any squabbling," said Mrs Easebrook soothingly. She was not one to interfere in anything and she didn't want to know who was in the right, either! Joey realized that the Easebrooks would be of no help. Victor knew it too.

"Give me my school bag!" he yelled.

But Ringo did not open the door. He sat in his bedroom softly brushing the whisks on the nearest cymbal, but he could hear what they were saying. Swish-swish, swish-swish, he went and at last Victor's assurance broke down.

"How about a little orange juice?" asked Mrs Easebrook.

By then Victor and Johnson had already retreated on to the street. Joey shut the door after them. He did not want orange juice, either. What did orange juice matter in a case of life or death?

Ringo opened the bedroom door and carried his drum set down to the cellar again. Victor's bag was lying on the bed pillow. Joey walked over to it purposefully. Now he would be able to prove who had stolen his bike and had taken it to pieces. But there was nothing in the bag except two rusty bells and a skirtguard for a lady's bike, nothing of Joey's. The whole performance had been pointless and there was nothing left to do but throw Victor's bag out of the window to Johnson who was waiting outside.

8

Katie was dreaming the loveliest dream: Olive had thrown a bicycle into the water, but it was not Joey's bike, it was a rusty old bike which Mrs Nettleton did not want because the gears had jammed. Joey had another bike, much redder and as alive as could be. It could run around by itself without anyone to push the pedals and it cycled itself sky-high, reeling along the edges of the clouds, just where the silver lining showed. Joey only had to whistle to make the bike come galloping back just like a dog. But then Joey gave his bike to Dad to ride.

Katie was smiling when she woke up, smiling among all her teddy bears. Woolly had curled up behind her ear, Bear-bear was stuffed under the pillow and she could feel Middle Ted's shaggy head under her arm. The cereal bowls gave a clink as they landed on the table in the kitchen and the spoons rang silvery against each other.

"Are you there, Mum?" called Katie.

"Yes, I'm up."

"Come and put your hand on my head and you'll

feel what a lovely dream I had! I'm dreaming everything the way it should be . . ."

Her mother ran up the stairs to put her hand on Katie's tousled head for a moment.

"Where's Joey?"

"He spent the night at Ringo's. He rang up and said he wouldn't be coming home. Something didn't go the way he wanted and it sounded as if he had troubles. I don't know what he's up to, but it's certainly something . . ."

Katie closed her eyes tightly, trying to see the bike on the edge of the clouds again, but it had already come tumbling down.

"What about the dream?" asked Mum.

"Can't feel it any more . . ."

Mum didn't ask any questions and luckily she had Charlieboy to bother about. He had got out of bed feeling cross and refused to be dressed. There was no question of washing, and any food which came his way was flung spinning through the air.

"You're not getting a cold, are you, little cross-patch?" Katie heard Mum say.

Katie lay where she was, remembering everything. The drowned bike – the cannibalized bike which Joey had not managed to get after all. Now Olive was beginning to poke her nose out of the cupboard. She came closer, determined to interfere.

"Go away," said Katie aloud. "Otherwise I'll tell Grannie!"

Mum had to leave for her mail delivery.

"Just leave Charlie in peace," she told Swan. "He can eat later if he feels like it. I'll pick up the mail and go to the furthest houses and deliver it. Then I'll come back and take care of Charlie."

Swan tried to protest. "I can't cope with him. You're the only one who's allowed to touch him!"

But Mum went, anyway. The door had only to slam shut for Charlie to start yelling again. Now the telephone was ringing as well and Katie had to answer. It was Dad.

"Hallo, how are you?" Dad asked.

"Charlieboy screams all the time," said Katie.

"Can I speak to Mum please?"

"She's just left."

"She's not at home?" said Dad, sounding as if he suspected the worst. "Did she have to go so early? I can never get hold of her!"

"Yes, she had to. Joey's not at home, either. He spent the night at Ringo's."

"Now why should he do a thing like that? He should be home at night. What's he doing there?"

"Perhaps it got late so he couldn't walk back," Katie suggested.

She should not have said that.

"There's no need for him to walk when he's got a bike. He could be home in a minute," said Dad. "He is taking care of that bike, isn't he? He doesn't leave it out and forget to lock it?"

Katie did not answer.

"Why aren't you saying anything? Are you there?"

"Yes."

"Where's Joey's bike? In the cellar?"

Katie wanted to put the receiver down but Dad stopped her.

"Well, don't you know where it is?"

"No . . ."

"Surely he wouldn't leave it outside in the street at the Easebrooks all night? It was the finest bike in the whole town! I bought it at the same bike shop I used to go and look in when I was a boy. In those days you couldn't get hold of a bike whenever you wanted one – not unless you were willing to starve to get it. I had extra gears added, too! Someone might take them off – people are stealing things left and right these days. It's not like it used to be when you could put the milk money out on the steps and no one took it except the person who was meant to. But of course Joey doesn't care about that. Does he take care of the bike?"

"Yes," said Katie, starting to cry. "Joey thinks his bike is the best in the world."

"There, then," said Dad. "There's no need for you to cry about it. I just want to be sure he looks after it. If he lets it get stolen I don't know what I'll do. But you needn't worry about it. That's Joey's business."

Katie put the receiver down and Swan had to pick it up. Then she rushed up to her room and stood there, thinking wildly. What should she do? This morning she had thought she would shut Olive in the cupboard before she went to school so that she didn't have to listen to her, but now she no longer dared to. Katie put on her shoes and coat before rushing out of the house. She didn't want to listen to any of Swan's conversation with Dad and if she had to be alone with Olive instead, it could not be helped.

Swan had to answer Dad's questions about what she had been doing during the week, why she had spent her time at the stables instead of going home and doing her homework. She was not to throw away her youth on some idiot in riding breeches! It would be better to stick to Peter.

Swan groaned as she listened to Dad. "Why didn't you say that a year ago?" she asked irritably. "When Peter was still living here, so that I could have gone on meeting him? This is a fine time to say it, when he's living three hundred miles away!"

"Yes, that's why I said it," said Dad honestly.

His 'phoning home didn't make anyone happy. On the contrary, thought Dad, his worst nightmares came true, it was impossible to get a sensible word out of anyone. And what about his own wife Sonia who couldn't even stay at home! He wanted to talk to Katie again to find out why she was crying, but Swan told him that Katie had already gone to school.

In fact Katie came back as soon as the 'phone call was over, went quietly up to her room, got out her old woolly cap, pulled it down over her eyes to hide her face and felt where her eyes were. She cut out two little holes in the cap. Then she went back to the kitchen and pulled out various drawers.

"What are you looking for?"

"Nothing . . ."

At last she found it, the round metal tube with a handle used for pushing out apple cores to make baked apples. The tube was the same size as a pistol barrel and if you felt it in your back you would certainly think you were being held up. Katie pushed the apple-corer into her pocket and walked slowly to school.

Swan was having a difficult time with Charlieboy. When Dad rang off she found that Charlie had got hold of a spoon and was trying to scoop his milk from the cat bowl under the sink. When he was picked up he struck out and yelled as if he were being kidnapped. He succeeded in wriggling loose and hit his forehead hard on a chair. Then he screamed

about that instead, with a different kind of furious yell, as if he had a special sound for every ill. At last Mum came home and Charlie brightened up, looking as pleased with himself as if he had got her back by his own efforts.

Swan went off to school, relieved. She had the first hour free but she did not want to risk more telephone conversations and bawling so she decided she might as well go to school early. She walked along thinking about Peter. She remembered how Peter had looked when he wanted her to kiss him behind a slot machine in a shop one day, and how they had caught sight of each other, she from the bus and he from the furniture van, when he was moving to another town. Was he as upset as I was, or wasn't he? Swan wondered. She would never know.

The school lay in silence when she reached it, the sun pouring in through the school door and gilding it like an altar panelling. She had arrived while the first class was still in session and there was not a soul in the school yard. Swan settled in the warmest corner of the doorway and closed her eyes. She recited to herself her latest love poem:

Heart, we must forget him,
you and I, tonight.
You forget the warmth he gave,
I'll forget the light.

When you've done it, tell me;
I'll stop thinking then.
Hurry! While you dawdle
I'm remembering him again . . .

Swan heard someone walking towards her. She looked up. It was Peter Moore.

"It's you!" he said.

They looked at each other as if they had never been parted. Slowly it dawned on them what a strange meeting this was, a mixture of fortune and wish fulfilment.

"I was just going in to get a copy of my records," he said.

"I arrived a bit early, I've got a free period," said Swan.

Both of them smiled.

"Stay here, I'll run up to the Head's office," said Peter.

There was no need for Swan to answer. He was gone; the magic was over. Was it true that Peter had been standing there only a second ago? That he had landed right in the middle of the last line of the poem? Why had she thought of that poem just then? Perhaps it was an omen? Swan went on sitting there, not daring to move.

Again there were footsteps. Surely Peter could not have come back from the office already? When Swan looked up. Alec was standing there – Alec, of all people! He was carrying his drawing pad.

"So there you are!" he said. "Did you come early, too?"

He stood opposite her in the doorway and began to draw her. Swan felt a chill in her heart. How could Alec come into the same scene without asking permission of her and Peter? What did it all mean? She saw Alec's drawing grow under his pencil. First he drew a square, then began to fill in her forehead, nose, mouth and chin, as if he had caught her in the little box. But the eye was crooked.

"My eyes don't look like that," said Swan.

Now Peter came back. There they stood, all three of them, not knowing what to do or say.

Five blocks away Katie was going into a post office. Not the usual post office where her mother worked but one further off. Katie had worked out for herself that it was the right thing to do, though she was not sure that Olive had wanted it. Katie had thought of it herself because if she was going to do as she planned she must at least be sure of not meeting her mother, who would certainly stop her. Katie had firmly made up her mind to get hold of some money somehow. She must! Dad must not be angry with Joey and Joey must not be without a bike.

"If I've been so stupid as to throw Joey's bike away I might just as well be a robber too," Katie told herself, with death in her heart. "I've only myself to blame!"

There was a long line at every counter window. Katie took her place in the nearest one, behind a woman holding a pile of envelopes. She looked at the back of the woman's checked coat. Katie would have to stay in the line until the woman reached the counter and when she took out her money to buy stamps Katie would pull her cap down over her face, take the apple-corer out of her pocket and press it against the middle blue check on the woman's coat

so that it felt like a pistol. Then she would say: "Hands up!" take the money and run. Katie laughed to herself as she thought about it. It was quite mad, but she was going to do it. Now another woman had come in and was standing behind Katie – a woman with a dachshund.

What am I to do now? Katie thought, very put out.

She had not planned on having other people in the line. The new woman was certain to notice that Katie was only holding an apple-corer, not a pistol!

"Please go ahead of me," Katie told the dachshund lady. "I'm not in a hurry. Your dachshund's legs may get tired!"

Surprised, the woman moved forward obediently. Katie looked for the spot where she would press the apple-corer on this new back. Below the scarf? No, it would be better not to touch the dachshund lady, because they had looked at each other. Katie had not yet pulled the cap down. In came a taxi-driver and an old man and took their place behind Katie. Katie waited until one more person had left the counter in front of them before saying, "Please go ahead!"

She stood behind the old man now, but she certainly wasn't going to frighten him. He might *die* of fright! Katie looked round helplessly. Was anyone else coming? Yes, a schoolboy was coming up behind her now, but schoolboys haven't any money. He must have come in for a stamp and she would have to change places yet again!

"Go ahead if you want to!"

Next came a man in a fur coat.

Katie's line moved forward slowly. The checked lady had not far to go and then came the dachshund lady, the taxi-driver, the old man and the boy. Katie looked round.

"Please go ahead of me," she said to the fur-coated man. "I don't mind waiting."

The fur-coated man stepped past her with his nose in the air.

Now I mustn't change any more, Katie decided.

The line began to move faster. The checked lady had to go to a different window, the dachshund lady only wanted to ask a question, the taxi-driver pushed a bundle of money through and got a receipt, the old man had to re-write his form and was sent away. Only the boy and the fur-coated man were left!

"What if he doesn't feel my apple-corer through the fur!" Katie was worried.

The second line beside Katie was not moving at all. It had been standing still all the time. The cashier in charge of it had gone off to check something. A raincoated man in the line was giving Katie a funny look as if to say: I'm going to be standing here all day! Katie wished she had stood at the back of that line instead.

How would she dare to prod the fur-coated man?

Suddenly the cashier for the second line came back and turned his notice round. Now that window was closed and everyone had to move over to Katie's line. The raincoated man stood right behind Katie. He would be able to see everything! But it was no good hesitating any longer.

Katie stood quite rigid with her hand in her pocket, clutching the handle of the apple-corer. Had she got her cap on? Yes, she had.

The schoolboy was leaving at last and the fur-coated man took a step towards the window. Slowly he took out a thick wad of money from his fat wallet and flicked through it. Slowly Katie pulled the cap down over her eyes. The apple-corer stuck crosswise in her pocket and would not come out. She had to tear it out and then she dropped it on the floor and could not find it. The eye-holes were in the wrong place.

"Don't push, child," said the fur-coated man.

Katie realized that she would never manage it. She

took a few shaky steps away from the line and tried to see the door through the cap, but the door had hidden itself away somewhere. She pulled off her woolly cap, ran out of the room as fast as she could go and hid behind the first door she could see, so that no one should hear how her heart was thumping.

9

"What actually are you up to?" asked the tall man wearing a raincoat who had been behind her in the line. He was looking round the door, smiling at Katie in a very friendly way.

Katie was so desperate that she could not manage a lie. "I was going to say 'Hands up!' but then I didn't dare!" she said.

The raincoated man laughed. "What was going to happen then?"

"I was going to poke this apple-corer in someone's back and take all his money," said Katie wearily. "It feels like a pistol."

"Are you sure about that?"

"No, but I think it does," said Katie humbly. "I haven't tried it yet."

The raincoated man laughed still more. He laughed very kindly, though, sometimes stealing a glance at Katie. Then he would start laughing all over again.

"I never heard anything so crazy," he said at last.

Katie had to laugh too.

"Yes, I really am silly," said Katie.

"You didn't think of doing a real robbery, did you?"

"Oh yes I did!" said Katie. "I did think that. Otherwise I wouldn't have cut holes in my cap. Look at it now!"

The raincoated man grew solemn. He stared at the cap and put his finger through one of the holes.

"Heavens above!" he said. "This might have been the perfect crime!"

They began to walk out of the post office side by side, the man keeping pace with Katie and giving her an anxious look from time to time.

"I saw you letting one person after another pass you in the line," he said. "I couldn't understand why. Didn't they have enough money?"

"No, they had all seen me," Katie explained. "And I was sorry for the old man, and the boy wouldn't have enough money. After all, you can't just rob anyone!"

"No, you're right about that," he said. "The man in the fur coat was the best choice."

"I was sorry for him too," said Katie. "He looked so funny. Why do you always have to be sorry for everyone? If you are it's hard to be nasty to them!"

"Wouldn't I do?" asked the raincoated man. "We could go back to the post office line and then I could come sauntering in, all unsuspecting. I don't mind being robbed. There's no need to be sorry for me!"

Katie had to laugh again. He was really very nice.

She ran obediently back to the post office and stood behind the door, gazing up at the ceiling and looking innocent.

In came the man, whistling. He took his place in the first line he came to, without looking round. Before Katie knew what was happening a woman had come in and taken her place behind him. Now the woman was in the way. Katie could not push ahead of her. What a fuss there would be! What was she to do now?

But the man had obviously noticed that the wrong person was behind him for he suddenly turned and raised his hat to the woman. "Please go ahead of me! I'm not in a hurry!"

He looked sideways in Katie's direction while the woman took a step forward, looking surprised. Katie would have to hurry up. Pulling the cap down over her eyes she strolled towards the man and prodded him in the back with the apple-corer.

"Hands up! Your money or your life!" she said.

The man put his hands up a little way, then took out his wallet and opened it so that his money was visible.

"Here you are, take it," he said.

Katie stared at him. There were a lot of coins in the wallet. She shook her head.

"No thanks, that's not nearly enough," she said. Then she began to cry, right there in the middle of the post office. She pulled her woolly cap over her mouth so that no one should hear her, but it was no use. The tears pushed their way out through the eye-holes while Katie quivered all over. The nice

man was very worried. He did not know what was going on.

"How much should it be then?" he said at last.

"Enough for a bike," wept Katie. "I threw my brother's bike in the river because he ate my pancake. And now I can never buy another one for him!"

At last the raincoated man had understood that it was not a game. Katie left him standing there and ran straight for home. When she arrived she caught hold of the door handle and stood there, gasping for breath. She was propping herself against it with both hands when her mother opened the door.

"So it's you out here! Come in, my little beetroot-face."

Katie followed her in through the door and trudged up to her bed where she collapsed on top of the covers, quite exhausted. She did not even look up when Mum came in.

Mum sat down beside her on the edge of the bed – just sat. She listened to Katie's breathing, jagged from crying, and then she began to stroke Katie's forehead, up towards the hair, over the head, over and over again. It felt as if she were smoothing out Katie's troubles and calming her thoughts inside her head. Soon Katie was breathing normally. She lay there waiting for each new stroke to come, feeling as if she were under a spell.

"Today I forgot to put two postcards in a letter-box and I had to go back again," said her mother. "Silly postcards which just said 'Wish you were here'. What have you been doing?"

"Nothing special," said Katie.

"Have you seen Joey?" asked her mother.

Katie moved her head unwillingly. "No."

She did not want to think about him.

"Joey's in trouble about something," said her mother, "but he won't say anything. I suppose he thinks it's something mothers couldn't understand."

Katie did not answer.

"I don't mind a bit, said the ball that got hit," said her mother. "As long as he gets through it all right.

But sometimes you have to worry. Remember one thing: if you ever do anything silly, something dreadfully silly, so silly that you don't even want to talk to yourself about it, do at least try telling me about it. However silly it is, I would try to help."

Katie looked up. "I've done it already," she said.

"Are you sure?" asked her mother.

Katie nodded.

"Is it dangerous?"

Katie shook her head.

"There we are then. If no one has been hurt it can't be all that important. Shall I guess what it's about?"

Katie gazed straight at her.

"Bird, fish or in between?"

"Fish," said Katie, smiling.

"Today, yesterday or last week?"

"The day before yesterday."

"Did you take something from the grocer's without paying?"

"No. Worse."

"Fish . . . Did you take a tin of sardines for the cat? Or a very big salmon that you didn't have room for up your sleeve so it flopped out on the ground and the police arrested you?"

Mum was smiling.

Katie shook her head.

"Worse. Worse."

Then Mum was serious again.

"Is it something to do with Joey? Something that can't be undone?"

Katie nodded breathlessly.

"Wait, it's something to do with water. It's something that happened the day before yesterday. You went out and swam with your coat on . . . You didn't . . . ? You couldn't have . . . ?"

"I did," said Katie. "I was so angry with Joey when he ate my pancake that I threw his bike into the water from the jetty. Then I couldn't get it out again and I don't know where it is and I daren't tell Joey because he'll go mad!"

Mum looked at Katie for a moment and then she began to smile. Then Katie smiled. Then Mum smiled even more and finally Katie could not help laughing – and then they both laughed crazily for a long time.

But then Katie began to cry again even when she was laughing. She said, "I didn't want to take anything from Grannie's bag . . . bikes are so expensive . . . and I tried to rob a nice man in the post office but he didn't have enough money! And Dad's going to be so angry with Joey and Joey's going to be so angry with me . . ."

"Nonsense," said Mum. "This is not the worst thing that's ever happened, it's just a bike that's been lost. Things are only things and they are never all that important. I was afraid it was something really bad. Do you know exactly where you threw the bike in?"

"Yes, but it's not there now," said Katie.

Mum jumped up and seized Katie's hand. She wanted to go and look at once. Perhaps she thought that Katie had not really searched properly. Charlieboy was awakened from his sweet slumbers and had to go with them in the stroller. They sped down to the river at full tilt.

"Aren't you cross with me?" asked Katie on the way.

"Well it was a silly thing to do," said Mum, "throwing a whole bike in just for the sake of an old pancake! What if I were to go chucking bikes in the water every time you ate my pancakes! There wouldn't be a bike left in the district. But there's not much point in being angry – I don't suppose you're planning to do it again?"

"Oh no!"

"Another time you must throw away your own things when you get angry, not Joey's."

"Then he shouldn't annoy me," said Katie.

"Perhaps he'll be more careful in future," said Mum.

They had reached the river but the stroller would not roll through the sand. Its wheels stuck. Katie had to stay with Charlie while Mum went across to the jetty. She seemed to think that the bike might be lying in fairly shallow water. Katie had to run over and point out the right place from the very end of the jetty and Mum suddenly got cross.

"Couldn't you have been satisfied with knee-deep water so that we could get it out? You might have controlled yourself a bit!"

"If I had I wouldn't have thrown it in at all," said Katie.

Mum lay down on her stomach on the jetty and peered into the water, but it was full of ripples and reflected clouds. It was impossible to see into it.

"Lucky I haven't been to the hairdresser's," said Mum, and hanging on to the edge of the jetty she

stuck her head down into the water. She came up again, with dripping hair, but without having seen a thing. Then she took off her shoes, rolled up her jeans and dropped her coat on the jetty so that she could take at least a few steps down the bathing ladder.

"It wasn't there!" shouted Katie. "It was straight off the end!"

"Am I really going to have to take all my clothes off?" grumbled Mum. She looked around. "No, it would be too awkward. I'm wet already, so I'll just have to swim in my clothes."

She jumped in off the end, jeans and all. Katie

thought that was splendid. Mum splashed about on both sides of the diving-board, ducking towards the bottom three times.

"Not there! Not there either!" screamed Katie. "Not so far out!"

But Mum could not hear her under water. Finally she emerged sufficiently for Katie to make herself heard.

"Closer, I said! You can stand there!" shrieked Katie.

Mum laughed her seagull laugh. She waded to just about where Katie was pointing, but there was neither sight nor feel of the bicycle.

"I told you it wasn't there any more," said Katie.

When Mum left the jetty she stubbed her toe on a boat-hook which was lying in the sand, almost invisible. If only she had found it a bit earlier, before she jumped in, she need not have got soaked through.

"Lying there without a word to say for yourself, you idle object!" said Mum. "What do you think you are, anyway?"

"It knows the bike's not there so it didn't want to get wet as well," said Katie.

Mum snorted. She wrung out her hair and squashed the coat into a bundle in the stroller. They jogged full speed for home while Katie recounted all her attempts to improve the situation – about the bike in the school yard and Olive's ideas about stealing from the handbag and the post-office robbery. Mum shuddered as she listened.

"You can't make a mistake better by making another one," she said.

"I had to do something!" said Katie.

"You should have told Swan at once, while the bike was still there. She could have got it out. Now we've got to work out what to do instead. You've got to tell Joey all about it so that he doesn't think up any stupid tricks of his own."

Katie nodded glumly.

Mum 'phoned Grannie as soon as she got home and told her the whole story from start to finish. Joey came in in the middle and she let him listen. He stared at Katie as if he had never seen her before.

"Was it YOU who took my bike?"

"Well, you took my pancake!" said Katie.

"Is there a soul in the world who knows how children can be so crazy?" said their mother on the telephone. "Quiet, so that I can hear what Grannie says."

"What does she say?" asked Katie.

"She says you get the children you deserve!"

10

"It's all your fault," Joey told Katie. "You're not supposed to touch my bike! We'll never find it again. Someone saw you throwing it in the river and took it."

"It wasn't only my fault," said Katie. "You're not supposed to shut me out and throw my bears around!"

"Both of you are in the wrong," said Mum. "Now forget it. The important thing is not whose fault it was but what we can do about it."

"We've already done everything we can do," said Joey. "I almost caught Victor committing bicycle theft, but it wasn't Victor who took my bicycle. He didn't have my bicycle parts."

"You can thank me for stopping you hitting him with your bat," said Katie, "because I hid it. Otherwise he would have died, all for nothing."

Mum got out the paper to see if there was anything about found bikes, but there wasn't. Then she rang the police lost-property department. They had hundreds of bikes there. She only had to explain what their lost bike looked like and then go and have a look. At least every other bike they had was red, the policeman said. Joey wanted to go there at once, and Mum was equally enthusiastic.

"Not that I know how the bike could jump out of the water and make its way right over to the police station," said Joey. "After all, thieves don't go to the police with their stolen goods."

"You never know," said Mum. "Trust in the unexpected! Perhaps it'll be standing there when we go in. Right in the middle, bright red and nothing much wrong with it."

"I'll believe that when I see it," said Joey.

"And you'll never see it if you don't believe it," said Mum. "Because that means you won't even go and have a look!"

Mum and Joey would have time to go to the police station in the lunch break but Katie had to go to school.

"And no post-office robberies on the way," said Mum. "This bike is going to be got back the right way or it will have to come by itself!"

Katie looked crafty. "What if I go back to school with Olive, though?"

"Then you must have a serious talk with her. You're the only person who can keep her in order!"

Katie took her other woolly cap, the one with no holes in, and set off for school, and sure enough, Olive popped up just round the corner. She only wanted to talk about what Dad was going to say when he came home, and she didn't believe that the bike would be at the police station either. Probably some speedboat had run over it so that the bike had got mixed up in the propeller and been carried right out to sea, said Olive. What should we do then?

"It's none of your business," said Katie.

She crossed the street to the school yard and zigzagged among the other children so that Olive could not follow her.

Lou was not there, she had mumps, and there was a lot of break time left. Katie had no one to play with so she stood by herself fingering the pieces of chalk in her pocket. Perhaps she should mark out hopscotch squares and play alone? Then she caught sight of Jump-jump over by the school doors. He rushed up

to them at top speed as usual and by the doors he stopped and jumped up and down in front of them, trying to push open one side of the door to go in. But it was no good because the door had to be pulled, not pushed. Jump-jump got so confused when it wouldn't open that he ran off again. Katie felt sorry for him and pushed through the crowd to see where he had gone.

Jump-jump was running to and fro along the fence on the other side of the yard. Katie stationed herself in one corner so that she would be there when he came back and when Jump-jump caught sight of her he stopped. He went on jumping on the spot and waved to her. Katie waved back. Then Jump-jump smiled and set off again, his head held high.

Katie drew a neat little chalk square on the asphalt yard before he came back again. She wrote *Hello* in the square. Jump-jump came back, saw it, and hopped even faster when he saw what was written there. Then he said "Hello" back again and rushed away.

Katie smiled to herself. She rubbed out *Hello* and wrote *My* instead and when he came back Jump-jump ran straight to the square and looked down. Before he came back again Katie had put in an arrow which pointed away from the rubbed-out square. She ran a little way off and drew a new square and wrote *name is* in it. Would he follow her? Yes, he did, he came tearing up and read the new words, but the school bell went at that moment! Katie didn't have a chance to make a square with her name in it, but now she was enjoying the game. She spent the

whole period thinking about the squares she would draw, and on the way home she looked for Jump-jump.

There he was! He had already run halfway to the grocer's, but he looked round from time to time. Katie wrote her name in a square and a little further off she drew an arrow. She drew one arrow after another as she walked along and just as she was drawing one of them Jump-jump came rushing past in the other direction. He was on his way to her name square to see what was written there.

She had to hurry then to keep ahead with her arrows! Jump-jump was much too quick for her. Before she knew it he was back again, looking dis-appointed because nothing else had been written. He rushed off and disappeared, while Katie drew her way home.

Mum and Joey were back again, having searched through two whole cellars full of bicycles, first one of boys' bikes and then one of girls' bikes as well in case Joey's had been put in there by mistake. But his bike was not there, it was not anywhere. Joey was lying on the bed in his room, refusing to speak to anyone.

Mum sent Katie out to the houses closest to the swimming place. She was to ring the door bells and ask if they had seen anyone take a bike out of the water. Katie dreaded it but her mother told her exactly what to say.

"It's not any worse than robbing the post-office line!" she said.

When Katie came out she noticed that Jump-jump was still about. He came rushing along, looking happy, but could not stop. Instead he ran past her four times, just to and fro. Katie had to draw a square for him although she was in a hurry, but before she could write anything Jump-jump was there again, putting on a spurt as he passed. He caught hold of her hand and took the chalk with him as he went.

"Stop that, it's mine!" shouted Katie, but she could not chase him because she had to go to the beach houses.

No one had seen Joey's bicycle, wet or dry. Katie told everyone who opened the door what her name was and asked them to write down her telephone number so that they could 'phone if they saw it. All of them wanted to know how the bike got in the water and Katie said that a silly boy had thrown it in and she joined in their remarks about "the wretched boy". A lot of people said: "Yes, that's what young people are like nowadays!" or: "They should be punished, that would teach them to leave other people's things alone!"

Katie walked home again, heavy-footed and wondering if she would even like a chat with Olive. But then she caught sight of the square she had drawn for Jump-jump. There was something written in it: *Mike*, it said in uneven lettering. What could it mean?

Then she understood.

"Did you know Jump-jump's name was Mike?" she shouted as she came through the door at home.

Joey was sitting, downcast, at the kitchen table.

"Of course I knew. He used to sit at the desk next to mine!" he said. "But I don't care about Mike! Have you heard anything about my bike?"

Joey was not particularly pleased to know that some people might 'phone if anything happened. Everything was just as bad as before. And tomorrow Dad would be home. Even Mum became quite solemn when she thought about it. What were they to do about him?

"Sooner or later he'll have to know," said Mum. "Shall we tell him the whole thing right away or shall we wait a little longer for the unexpected to happen, and hope the bike will come back so that we don't have to upset him?"

"I think Katie should tell him," said Joey. "She'll have to say she was the one who threw it in."

"In that case you'll have to tell him how you annoyed her too, of course," said Mum. "And that the bike was unlocked."

They all looked at each other. It was not going to be easy to explain about the very best bike in town, a bike with extra gears and all.

"Shall I ask Olive what to do?" asked Katie.

Mum looked tempted but she checked herself.

"No thanks. At least he's not going to hit us, he'll just rage around for twenty minutes and we shall have to put up with that, since you've been so silly. The worst thing is that he'll be so disappointed . . ."

Swan came home just in time to hear all their troubles. Then she told them about her afternoon. She had wandered round the town with Peter and Alec and then they had gone to the stables together. Peter had tried to get a free ride on a horse called Stamper and Alec had drawn Peter as a clown. Finally they had gone to the station with Peter and just as the train was going out Peter said that his hands were frozen in the winter because he had no mittens. He only wanted green mittens with red fingers, he said. Any other kind of mitten gave him the creeps. He had once had such a pair . . .

"You'll have to knit yourself another pair," said Alec, who had no idea what mittens they were talking about. Alec had not been in Swan's class in the year when the green and red mittens she had knitted in handicraft were ready just in time for Peter's birthday.

"There's probably some female on the train who could teach you to knit," Alec had added.

"But then I drew a mitten for Peter in the dirt on the train window," said Swan.

"Peter?" said Mum. "Are you talking about Peter Moore?"

Swan laughed and danced round.

"Yes, who else? You yourself said the time of miracles wasn't over yet and to trust in the unexpected! Peter was actually trying to get a summer job here."

Joey heard what they were saying and was furious.

"Stop talking about Peter and Alec!" he yelled. "You ought to be talking about my bike! Can you promise that I can trust in the unexpected? Can you?"

"Of course I can!" said Swan. "I really thought I would never see Peter again, so you see! From now on I shall trust in the unexpected and I think you should do the same. Expect Dad not to be as cross as you think he will be – that would be totally unexpected!"

11

Dad was due home on the four-ten train. Mum was going to cook his favourite dishes for dinner, spare ribs of pork and cauliflower. Swan laughed when she heard about it.

"Spare ribs on an ordinary weekday! That might look suspicious," she said.

Joey wanted Mum to buy him a new bike before Dad came home. He and Katie could work the price off by helping in the house all year, he thought – especially Katie. But Mum was not having that.

"We'll wait till Dad gets home and have a family council about the bike, that's the only thing to do," she said. "It will be quite exciting, much better than a TV thriller, because you always know how that's going to end."

"You promised to help us however silly we've been," Katie reminded her.

"I know," said her mother.

"Three against one is cowardly," said Swan. "I'm going to support Dad. He wasn't the one who made this mess."

Katie nodded. Olive had tried to stick her nose in and say it was Dad's fault too that the bike had been thrown in the river, since it was he who had been teaching Katie how to make pancakes. But Katie had locked Olive in the wardrobe.

Joey shrugged his shoulders. All he could do now was to become like tough Victor who didn't give a hang for anything, or the sheriff who looked danger in the eye without blinking. Either, or. What happens, happens, he thought.

On the way to school Katie noticed that Jump-jump had been there before her. She saw strange arrows outside the fence and when she followed them she came to a crooked square with a house in it. And a little further on a square which said *School*. He was obviously laying a trail so that she could find her way to school easily.

Katie wanted to draw some arrows too, but Jump-jump had taken her chalk. When she reached the school, there he was, jumping up and down, but he vanished through the door as soon as he saw her wave. Katie asked the teacher for a few chalk stumps in the very first break.

At lunchtime Jump-jump drew arrows and a whole lot of squares with numbers in them to be added together and you found the answer in the last square you reached. Katie drew a trail that led to a square which said "We'll go on after school," but someone had smudged the square before Jump-jump arrived.

Katie came out into an empty school yard after the last period. Jump-jump had already gone, of course,

not having seen her message. But up by the grocer's, Katie found a long, new, crooked arrow – one that had been drawn since yesterday. She began to follow the new trail and when she turned the corner by a strange house Jump-jump was standing right in front of her, laughing as he hopped. He had already drawn the next arrow and that was what he was jumping on now.

"Hello, Katie," he shouted, and ran. But then Katie began a trail of her own in a different direction to see if he would notice and follow it. At last he did, but after a while Katie began to wonder how late it was and whether it was time to go home to the family council and cauliflower. She crossed out the arrow she had just drawn and drew a new one pointing towards home, with a square with a bicycle inside it as an explanation. She wanted to show him that she had to go home and have a serious talk about bikes.

But Jump-jump had no intention at all of stopping. He came rushing back and crossed out Katie's last arrow as hard as he could until it was just a smudge. Instead he drew a long, fine, new arrow in his direction and stamped commandingly on it when Katie came in sight. She was forced to follow a little further. Jump-jump's trail led past Park Street, down the hill and into the woods. Where the asphalt ended he began to scratch arrows on the pine-needle path with sticks. He was a long way ahead of her now but she could still see him. There he stood, behind a fir tree, beside a bike. He obviously wanted to show her what a bike looked like! Ignoring the remaining arrows, she ran ahead.

The bike was red with upswept handlebars like nickel-plated reindeer horns. It had extra gears. The saddle looked like a plastic loaf. It was Joey's bike! It couldn't be anything else! Joey's discarded, drowned bike had risen from the depths of the river and stood glittering under Katie's very eyes!

Jump-jump bounced with delight.

"Where did you get it?" screamed Katie.

"I saw you push it in. I pulled it out!" said Jump-jump.

"How could you?"

"With the boat-hook!" Jump-jump laughed. "I'm very strong."

"What are you going to do with it?" asked Katie.

Jump-jump stopped a moment and clutched the handlebars. It looked as if he intended to keep it.

"It's Joey's bike," said Katie.

Jump-jump nodded. "I know Joey. We're best friends," said Jump-jump.

Katie wondered if Joey knew that. Perhaps Jump-jump thought they were because they had sat next to each other, but that had been some years ago. Katie took hold of the bike, but Jump-jump began to push it away.

"Aren't you going to give it back to Joey?"

"Oh yes," said Jump-jump. "In a minute. I'm going to ride it first."

They looked at each other and Katie began to tell him about Dad and the pancake and the whole mix-up. Jump-jump just hopped and nodded. Then he grabbed the handlebars and spun the bike round.

"Come on!" he shouted.

Off they went, out of the woods together, with the bike. The further they ran the more obvious it became that they were on the way home to Park Street.

Jump-jump was going to give Joey back his bike! Katie was so happy that she had to jump up and down too, just like Jump-jump. They were not far from Katie's gate when Joey came walking by. He stopped as if he had seen a ghost, then ran towards them.

"Let go of my bike!" said Joey. "What do you think you're doing with it?"

Jump-jump turned quite pale, dropped the bike as if it had burned him and ran away.

Katie hit Joey as hard as she could. How could he be so stupid?

"You idiot! He pulled it out of the river for you! He was watching when I threw it in!" she shouted. "Run after him and tell him! He was just being kind!"

Joey looked crestfallen. "I'll never catch up with him . . ."

"You can ride your bike, can't you?"

Joey jumped on to his fiery steed and set off at top speed down the road. Of course he would catch up with Jump-jump.

But Katie walked on, slowly at first, towards home. The surprise had not caught up with her yet. She had to wait for it and move a foot at a time while she was thinking it all out. What luck it was that Jump-jump had seen her on the jetty and how strange that he had managed to get the bike out! Then Katie began to run. She must go home at once and tell the others about the surprise of the century!

Once home, she went straight to the kitchen and jumped on the counter beside Mum who was just serving the spare ribs. It all looked mouth-wateringly good and there was apple sauce on the table as well. There was a mild but definite smell of cauliflower.

"If he asks why we're having spare ribs on a day like this we might just as well tell him at once," said Mum. "Remember that, even if the food ends up on the floor!"

"You can throw the silly old spare ribs away!" said Katie. "Joey's bike has come back!"

12

Dad opened the door down below and shouted as he generally did: "Ho-ho! Anyone at home?" Everyone answered at once except Joey who was still out. Dad went to the bathroom and washed his hands. He was rather late but it didn't matter because the dinner was late too.

"Where have you been all this time?" asked Mum, on behalf of the dinner.

"There was three minutes' delay at one of the stations," said Dad, "but we made up for it on the final run. I've been at the bicycle shop, looking for locks for Joey's bike. An ordinary lock is not much good. If he can't lock the bike onto something else, anyone passing could just pick it up, put it in a truck and drive off with it."

Mum's face did not move. She just gave a hasty thought to what a lock would look like if there were no bike to put it on – but now there was a bike! "Perhaps he could keep his bike under his bed at night and lock it to the bed leg so that he wouldn't start riding it in his sleep?" said Mum suddenly.

"You can never be careful enough with bikes . . ."

Dad gave her a thoughtful look. "You're teasing me already," he said. "I suppose you don't think there are any bike thieves or light-fingered gentlemen around here? I suppose you believe that every bike has its own little guardian angel keeping it safe from all evil?"

"I don't really know what I think," said Mum. "I was just wondering."

Katie took a closer look at Mum. What had come over her now? Was she going to give everything away although there was no need?

"Mmmm, that smells good!" said Dad. "Well bless my soul, cauliflower in parsley sauce! It's not my birthday, is it? No, it isn't. Have you started blowing your fortune on food? We can't have Sunday dinner every day of the week, can we?"

"Of course we can," said Mum. "If it's good, it's good, even on a week day. Taste it and you'll see. Spare ribs and cauliflower rise above good and evil, just like the sun . . . Who said I wasn't allowed to cheer you up on week days?"

"Grandmama," said Dad. "She's turning in her grave this minute. If I took more meat than potatoes I would never get to heaven, she would say. And you were never allowed to eat much fish, or much potato either for that matter. 'Enough is as good as a feast,' she used to say."

"That was quite right," said Mum, "in her day. But we're living in my day now, so help yourself!"

"You're not afraid of having a good time, are

you!" said Dad. "You think anything goes as long as it's fun . . ."

Mum nodded and Dad helped himself to a spare rib. One to start with and then a lot more. He ate it as if he were ravenous.

"I expect you think I've earned this," said Dad. "Guess why it took me such a long time to buy the lock."

Mum shook her head.

"Well, there was a fellow ahead of me in the shop who wanted to know what boys' bikes cost these days. I told him they cost an awful lot. He was thinking of buying a bike for some lad he didn't even know as it turned out, so I asked, tactfully you know, what gave him the idea."

"What did he say?" asked Mum.

"He had the idea that he'd like to do a good deed," said Dad with surprise. "He had been practically robbed at the post office by some little girl who wanted his money to buy a bike for her lout of a brother! Kids are absolutely crazy these days!"

Mum and Katie stared at Dad without answering.

"I asked him why he hadn't arrested her and he said he hadn't had the heart. On the contrary, he had encouraged her and was going to let her have some money! People are so silly! How are kids ever to learn what's right if they are allowed to do what they like and get away with it?" said Dad.

"Justice should be tempered with mercy!" said Mum, quivering. "Haven't you ever heard that?"

"That's just what I thought you'd say," said Dad. "But I told him he ought to be more careful. He could ruin that girl by making things so easy for her. She'll go round robbing folks all day long!"

"Oh no," said Katie, under her breath.

"This fellow said he had thought it was a game. He had tried to excuse himself because he didn't realize it was serious. But then she began to cry and said the money wasn't for her, it was for her brother. He was probably the one who sent her."

"Now wait a minute," said Mum, "there's no need for that! You don't know anything about it."

"I know what boys are like," said Dad. "It was probably some useless boy who had broken his bike and couldn't be bothered to put it together again. So he sends his sister off, if it was his sister, and forces her to rob people! All I can say is that if I heard you were doing things like that for your boyfriend, I don't know what I'd do," said Dad, turning to Swan.

Swan jumped. But then she lifted her head and stared back at him. "Me! Do you think I'd agree to just anything? If I can refuse you, I can refuse my boyfriends too! I don't go around with little gangsters, remember? Are we going to have another of our incredibly stupid, matter-of-life-or-death squabbles now, or shall we eat our dinner? What's it going to be?"

Katie froze. Dad drew himself up. Mum hid her face in her hands. Then she burst out laughing.

"Calm down, Swan, let Dad finish. It's so thrilling, you could die."

Dad sighed. "I told this fellow that he should give up going round buying bikes for little ruffians he doesn't know. If the boy had ruined his bike it was his own fault, I said. It would serve him right for not taking care of it. Bikes cost a fortune these days and kids have to learn to take care of things!"

"Shouldn't they learn to do good deeds, though?" asked Mum. "Shouldn't they ever see a good deed in their lives or meet a gentle, understanding person?"

"But he was ridiculous," said Dad. "He didn't even know where the kid lived! He was thinking of buying the bike on the off-chance and taking it along to the school – as if he could find his robber-girl among a whole lot of young villains! I had to warn him not to make such an idiot of himself!"

"Did he do his good deed or not?" said Mum.

"Did he buy the bike or not?" shouted Katie. "Come on, tell us!"

"No idea," said Dad. "I wasn't going to stand there all day chatting to a stranger once I'd bought the lock!"

Katie jumped to her feet, threw down her fork, which landed on Dad's plate, and rushed to the front door. Before they could stop her she had disappeared.

"What's up with her?" said Dad.

"Don't worry about it," said Mum. "We'll find out later. So is that the end of the story? Are we allowed to speak now?"

"Not really," said Dad. "I was going on thinking about that crazy man until I got to the grocer's. I had to go in and buy an evening paper just to talk to someone sensible, so I told your friend in there. She had to admit that I was right, if things were as they were, she said."

"Yes, that's just the point. Why didn't you come straight home to us instead?"

"Because, fool that I am, I went back to the bike shop," said Dad. "I planned to tell the fellow he could do as he liked as far as I was concerned, that is if I was wrong. After all, it might be some lad without a father who would never be given a bike in his whole life otherwise. Is that what you wanted to hear?"

"Oh yes!" cried Swan and her mother together.

"That's what I thought," said Dad. "But the bike shop was shut so it was a waste of time. 'Look after yourself and devil take the hindmost,' they used to say, and it's true. But I certainly did earn this dinner!"

13

Katie flew out of the door like a little fly on the end of a fishing line. She had to reach the shop before the raincoated man bought that bike! After all, Joey couldn't have two bikes! But then she jumped and stopped as if she had got hooked on something; Dad had told the man not to buy anything. Perhaps he had obeyed Dad and gone away! What was she running for?

But what if he was a stubborn man who had already made up his mind? Someone who absolutely had to throw his money around? There he would be with his bike, not knowing what to do with it. Katie started running again.

Then she stopped. Perhaps the man had already gone home. Then she ran. Perhaps he was looking all over the school yard now! Katie had to laugh at herself and her stops and starts. She began to rush-stop-rush on purpose until the whole business turned into a game, but she was going to the bike shop whatever happened.

It was locked and bolted.

Katie stood at the window for a time wondering what to do. Perhaps she should walk on the squares along the pavement, run five squares forward and then hop into the next on one leg, over and over again. No, she was tired of running. But she could step in the squares without looking to see where her foot went and if she didn't land on a single line she would hit on the solution in the end – the solution to the vanished bike-buyer. She strode on down the street.

She was not surprised to find herself getting closer and closer to school, because the street ran exactly in that direction and the paving stones knew quite well where to take her. She did not have to look.

"What am I supposed to be thinking out now?" Katie wondered to herself. "Oh yes, I know! What am I to do with much too nice men and much too many bikes?"

She had to stop in a square and grin to herself, but when she looked up again she saw Joey and Jump-jump in the school yard. Joey was teaching Jump-jump how to ride a bike, but she could see from a long way off that he wasn't getting on very well. Just then Joey picked up the bike and swung his leg over it. He was obviously going to show Jump-jump how to do it. Oh, misery and gloom! She looked down and saw she had stepped on a line. She was not supposed to look. She had broken the spell. Now she would never find the answer.

"Hello there! What are you up to?" said a man beside her. Katie looked round.

He was not standing at the end of the pavement

waiting, as she had imagined to herself. Instead he was bicycling along the street beside her, on a new, blue bicycle. Katie stopped short. There was nothing else to do.

"Don't you recognize me?" said the man.

"Oh yes," said Katie. "I'm the one who dreamed you here before I stepped on a line."

"I shall never believe that," said the raincoated man, "because I'm the one who's been riding around looking for you. I've been at it for nearly an hour, so it's lucky you came. Otherwise I would have kept the bike myself! I'm just beginning to take to it."

Katie did not answer. Perhaps that was the solution.

But the man went on, riding slowly alongside her as Katie walked directly towards the school yard. Joey was still there, riding circles round Jump-jump, who was hopping up and down. The red bike's antlers glittered brightly.

"Weren't you the one who wanted a bike for your brother?" said the man at Katie's side.

"Yes," said Katie.

"Was it true that you had thrown his away?"

"Yes," said Katie, still waiting to find out what the solution was going to be.

"But you didn't do it on purpose?" he asked.

"Oh yes, I did," said Katie, "but then I wanted to turn it all back again, but it didn't work."

"I don't want you to have to go round robbing people to make things all right again," said the man. "That's why I wanted to help. Now I've bought this bike, so everything will be as if it had never happened."

"Oh, oh, yes, yes," said Katie. She could not think of anything else to say. It would have been better if the first bike had stayed at the bottom of the river a little longer. How could you ever know what some stranger might make possible.

"What did you say?"

"Are you always as kind as this?" asked Katie.

"No, this is my first attempt!"

"Do you really want to give it away to just anyone?"

"No, not to just anyone. Only to someone who really needs it," said the man. "Only to your brother."

Katie looked again at the yard where Joey was still riding his bike. He was riding, oh, how he was riding, in beautiful big figures of eight. Jump-jump had drawn back a little so that he would not be run over.

"Where is your brother?"

Katie could feel Olive nudging her. She had sneaked out of the wardrobe. "Over there," said Katie, "in the yard."

"Which of them is it?"

"The one who's jumping up and down!" said Katie, giving Olive a push. "Jump-jump!" she shouted.

Jump-jump caught sight of her and waved. The man began to ride towards him, with Katie running alongside, giving him a push.

"Off you go!" she shouted.

When the man was going the right way Katie turned and stood in front of Joey, who almost ran her down.

"Watch out!" shouted Joey angrily.

But Katie rushed round and climbed on the back.

"Ride home," she hissed, "quick! Dad has been there for ages!"

Joey turned his head. He did not look pleased. Katie was much too heavy to be given a ride.

"I can't give rides to someone as big as you," he said.

"Just to the other side of the school yard and round the corner! Quick! Quick!" said Katie again.

"All right then, but only because you helped me get the bike back," said Joey.

He put his weight on the top pedal and kicked off as hard as he could. Olive threw herself into it as well, Katie could feel her there, perched behind her, but she did not dare to look round. Slowly the bike began to move.

"Faster, faster! This is a gangster chase!" Katie hissed at Joey.

He had got up speed now. Joey loved riding fast. They rushed away towards the school gate as fast as they could possibly go.

"Has Dad said anything yet?" Joey asked over his shoulder.

"Oh yes, oh yes, you'll hear about it later. He's bought you a special lock!"

Joey pedalled hard.

"You're nice now," Katie told Olive. "We thought of that at the same time!"

"What do you mean, nice?" asked Joey.

"I wasn't talking to you," muttered Katie.

"I shan't tell about you throwing it in the water," said Joey, "as long as no one else says anything."

Katie was being joggled on the hard rack. She had to hang on tight to Joey when he swung round a corner.

"Let me off, I'll run the rest of the way," said Katie.

Joey stopped.

"You mustn't bike ahead of me," said Katie, catching hold of the bike. "We must get home at the same time."

Joey snorted, but he set off very slowly so that Katie could keep up.

"Let go of the bike," was all he said. "I'm not going to ride away from you."

Katie laughed as she ran, light as a little fly soaring off through the air. Not like a fly on the end of a fishing-line, but like a real fly that can fly at fifteen miles an hour. She didn't care what the man was going to say to Jump-jump; it was up to them to divide the bike up as they liked. He himself had said that he wanted to be kind and that someone who needed the bike should have it.

In the doorway they met Swan, carrying her drawing-pad and wearing new earrings. You could see at once that she was going to meet Alec and would be home late.

"Hurry up, the food's getting cold," she said, before Joey could open his mouth.

Dad had finished eating and gone up to the living-room, where he sat in peace and quiet while the rest of the family stuffed themselves with spare ribs and cauliflower. There was ice cream to follow. Mum was going round humming, looking extremely pleased with life. When Katie took the fork out of her mouth and told her what had happened with the bicycle man and Jump-jump, she just laughed.

"I thought everything would turn out all right," she said. "If he just thinks about it, the man will be able to make sure the bike is put to good use. It's a pity we don't know his name because the unexpected that sometimes happens is often something inside someone else. Have you noticed? It's in them, right in the middle, like a little doodle on a page –

something unexpectedly nice. Come on, eat up so Dad can hear the end of the story."

"Yes, but what about the beginning of the story?" said Joey.

"I've already told him that," said Mum.

Katie took her ice cream up to the living room where Dad was sitting in the red chair with the soles of his feet touching on the floor so that Katie had room to sit between his knees. When Katie had made herself comfortable Dad said, "Now tell me the story again. I want to make sure I understand what really happened."

"I'll tell you my story as soon as I have finished eating," said Katie happily.

But what was the end of the story? Was it that Jump-jump was going to get a new bike from the tall man, or was it just that the best bike in the world was back where it belonged, and they could tell a story with a happy ending after all?